LIFE ALTERER

C. Yvette Spencer

LIFE ALTERER

C. Yvette Spencer

DRAMA NOVELIST

This is a Busybee Publication

busybee
PUBLICATION

ISBN-13: 979-8-9866848-0-2

To my readers:

✢✢✢✢✢✢

Thanks for choosing:

LIFE ALTERER

I enjoy creating rememberable characters and this book has a lot of them. Some I love, many I loathe. Some are soft and subtle, others are loud and colorful, but they all made this story great. In this book, Mildred is one of my favorites because she's so lively.

I'd love to learn which were your favorite. Let me know at:
C.yvettespencer@gmail.com

Let the peace of God operate in your hearts and minds. And remember, the only help God needs from you is faith. Stay prayed up, my friends.

_____

_____

_____

_____

C. Yvette Spencer

DRAMA NOVELIST

< Book Features >

A Note From the Author

My Lord and Savior have been there through it all. My journey will always start and end with my praise and worship of Him.

I also would like to express a huge thanks to my editor, Richelle McFate. She is absolutely amazing and is always there for me. May you always receive all that you give and more.

This story that was conceived with a single thought took three years to land upon the pages of a document and another two years to complete. It wasn't written lightly, but with the help of the Lord to assure that delicate topics were carefully written with no intentions to offend, but in hopes that this story will enlighten, awaken, and educate the reader to understand with compassion and sympathy, and to be taken empathetically. I pray that this book will touch readers and change them in the most philosophical way. If only one is reached and moved in the right direction from their position on the matter of racism, then my job will have been done.

Had I written this book when it was conceived in 2017; it would not have been as relevant as it is today. In the year 2022, hatred seemed to grow faster than the word love, projecting upon us a vengeful deadly force; literally using the deeds of the young to murder scores of people at a time, many in the name of racism. This book, even before it was published, was deemed worthy of banning by those who want us to bury the dialogues of the past. They cover them up with the delusion of cultural issues, political exploitation, and lies.

I am proud that this story was put in my heart, and even more ecstatic about its completion, so that I may share it with you who have an open mind and the gift of empathy. Enjoy, learn, and embrace what is to come in this story. Don't just read it and store the book away, discuss it with another, pass it on to the next, or gift someone a copy because the vital need of these topics must never be silenced, and their journey must never end.

C. Yvette Spencer

DRAMA NOVELIST

ACKNOWLEDGEMENT

I try to make each book a tab bit personal by honoring someone I know in some special way. Although I try to create unique characters, I often use family names or a name that has been given to me by a friend when my mind grows blank. I would like to take the time to acknowledge the names in this book and tell you where they derived from.

The name...

Walt / Tondey –I borrowed the name Walt from Walter Gaines. He's tall and dark like the main character Tondey in this story. When I envisioned Tondey, I thought of Walter, but just a little shorter. So, I guess you can say, I borrowed two pieces of Walter Gaines to form a couple of characters in this story. Walter Gaines is married to my mother's first cousin, Sara Gaines. Thanks to you both for the use of his name.

Paty- Paty is the name of my nephew's wife, Paty Anderson. When I described the character, I thought of Paty's long dark hair that always flow down her back. Although the character in this story is a mixed slave, Paty is a Mexican American. Thank you, Paty for allowing me to use your name.

Adessa – I wanted a name not used every day and that was relevant for the time period to describe this character. For resources, I turned to a co-worker by the name of Ann-Marie Dawson. She tossed about four names to me before delivering this perfect jewel for this character. Thank you, Ms. Dawson.

Chapter 1

~~~2018~~~

In the deep south of Alabama, good ol' country boy Roy, the passenger of a white 1980 F-150 Ford pickup, spotted an old Black man walking on a sidewalk in their small town. "Look at that old geezer."

"Who?" Walt, the driver, grip tightened on the steering wheel as his head swiveled around. A drizzle of goo ran down his chin, evidence of the chocolate tobacco he perpetually kept wadded behind his front lip.

"That old dark man. The one right there on the left. On the sidewalk." Roy pointed. "The trench coat. It's a hundred degrees, and he's wearing a long black coat."

"Oh, that old dark smut. I see 'im." Sitting up straight and wiping the juice from his chin with the back of his hand, Walt locked his fingers around the steering wheel and leaned forward. "Yeah, I see that smut." His eyes homed in on the old man like he was hunting prey. "Let's go get 'im." He pressed down on the gas pedal.

"Walt, wait!" Roy grabbed the dashboard just as Walt slammed on the brakes.

Right in front of his big white pickup was a short young Caucasian mother glaring at Walt from the street. Her fingers gripped her six-year-old's hand so tightly it had turned pale.

Walt looked up at the red traffic light then leaned his head out the window. "Um sorry, Leanne."

Furious, Leanne tightened her grip without noticing the wince of pain she caused her child. "You almost hit us, Walt!"

"Um sorry."

"C'mon." She yanked her daughter's hand, and they continued crossing the street.

"Damn. How's that for you? We ain't got but one light in town, and it decides to do its job today of all days."

A block ahead, the frail old man edged up to the road in leather-booted feet beside a parked sedan. He carefully settled a tall wooden staff into the gutter, preparing to step off the sidewalk.

"What's that he got on his shoulder?" Walt leaned forward to see.

"Whatcha call it? Like one of those bags. Like an old worn-out leather satchel. He's ancient."

They laughed.

"Old geezer." Walt looked at the light. "C'mon, man, turn green. He'll be on the other side of the street by the time you change."

"You know this light has always been slow."

They watched the old man slowly shift a boot with measured precision into the road and then pause to contemplate his next move. He did not look nor see the light had turned green.

"'Bout time." Resting an elbow on the door of the truck, Roy grabbed the top frame of the open window. "Go, go, go, go. Time it right. Time it right."

"Why's he stopping?" Walt slowed down.

"I'on know." Roy leaned forward. "What's he doing?"

The old man turned his staff's head in the direction of the road, as if to point the way, before leveling his other boot into the street.

Walt sped up.

"Not too fast, Walt, time it right."

"I got it. That's right, old man, c'mon in the street. Yeah, that's it." Walt fixated on the old man.

Another step and the old man had abandoned the curb. Failing to look left or right, he didn't see the F-150 bearing down on him.

As Leanne helped her daughter into the car, the roar of Walt's truck engine turned her in its direction. "Oh, God, Walt's gonna hit that old man. Hey, watch out for that truck!" Her warning drew the attention of others, but not the old man who kept on creeping further into the street.

"Here comes nigger juice." The truck moved faster, playing dramatic music with its thunderous engine. "Die, nigger, die!" Walt swerved in the direction of the old man who never saw the truck swipe his way.

The old man's body plowed into the vehicle behind him. His head bashed against its window.

As Walt sped away, he looked into his side-view mirror and spewed out a thick chunk of tobacco. "That's one way to kill a mockingbird."

Roy climbed halfway out the passenger window and waved a confederate flag. "White power!"

The truck made a quick turn down another street and disappeared from the townspeople's view.

As Leanne hurried into her car, the old African American man pushed away from the car and regained his balance. With his staff to support him, he again failed to look both ways and continued his journey across the road. He tapped his staff against the pavement until he reached the other sidewalk, and then slowly strolled on his way.

Later that evening, vehicles of all makes, dates, and models parked outside a high-roofed barn that nestled hidden away in the deep woods of Alabama. Inside the old, abandoned-looking wooden construction, Walt and Roy mixed in with a rowdy crowd of White men, all actively listening as a leader spoke with a thick country accent.

"Remember, no matter how bad you wanna get 'em—and believe me, I can appreciate your passion—we have to be careful. Walter, I saw you almost hit one today."

The men closest to Walt patted him on the shoulders while others applauded.

With a jaw swollen with chewing tobacco, he proudly received their praises with a wide grin. He turned to the speaker. "It's just Walt, sir."

"What?"

"My name's Walt. Not Walter. It stands for commander. A family name. One I carry with pride."

"Walt." The speaker slowly shook his head. "Yeah, as I was saying, I saw you almost hit one today."

The crowd cheered him again.

"Wait a minute before we go thinking it's alright to run over a nigger in the middle of the road with a town full of witnesses waiting to go blab to our nigger-loving sheriff. Walt, how'd you expect us to keep you out of jail with a whole town of fingers pointing your way?"

"I'll kill them too."

The crowd laughed.

"From where, jail?" He looked out in the crowd. "I know we all have those certain urges to kill a nigger. But with two dead Blacks killed upstate by White cops, and a Black woman raped and killed a skip town over, it would behoove us to keep a low profile for a spell. We all wish times were like they used to be when our grandpappies ran things, but they ain't. It's 2018. We got the right president for the right time. It took a long time, but we're finally under a leader who gets our thinking. That doesn't mean we're free to go out and kill whoever and whenever we want. We have to take it easy for a spell."

"What about our annual ritual? We still lynching one this year?" a voice from the crowd questioned loudly.

A cacophony of supporting words followed. Everyone's eyes fell on the leader, eager to hear his response.

"Oh, no. Make no mistake about it. Nothing, and I mean absolutely nothing, will ever stop our annual lynching." He pointed to his temple, his words gaining energy that meant to rally the crowd. "But we must think smart. We can't do a thing that'll draw attention to us. Keep cool heads. Go home, take care of your beautiful women and your darling babies, and remember, we are the superior race!"

The crowd became boisterous.

He raised a fist. "Every man, every woman, every boy, and girl live at our will!"

"You got that right!" a man's voice rose above the rabble.

"They work because the White man provides the jobs!" the leader continued.

"Yeah!" many yelled.

"They have food in their bellies 'cause we grow the crops and raise the cattle! They have roofs over their heads because the White man grows the trees and owns the factories! They call us the blue-eyed devil—we ain't no devils, we're their gods 'cause we supply their needs!" He stepped from behind the podium, lifted his head high, and took in the crowd's excitement.

Armed men loaded with moonshine, hard liquor, cigars, marijuana, and beer cheered with raised weapons, drinks, and fists.

"The White man is God's greatest creation! Our women are God's greatest art! That's why the Black man burns with desire for 'em. They are the goddesses of all women!"

"Yeah – Yes – You got that right! – Woo-hoo – Goddess!" Voices roared over one another.

"Now, let's get home to their good cooking and the kisses of our little ones. Until we meet again, stay true to the brotherhood. And remember, thinking is banking knowledge." Concluding as he did every meeting, he raised a fist into the air and yelled into the microphone. "Can I hear it? Hail to our people! Hail to our cause! Hail to the White Man! Hail to Trump! MAGA STRONG!"

"White Power!" A few added.

After the meeting, several members lingered in and around the barn. They periodically replaced cigars between their lips with jars of moonshine, whiskey, and beer.

Amicable conversation and laughter filled the night air. Some bragged about family, others complained about work, and a few voiced how much they hated anyone who didn't have the pure blood of the White man.

"So, Walt, you almost got one?" John Jr's big gut stuck out from his stout body like he was with child.

"One extra step and black nigger juice would've been splattered everywhere. Came that close." He showed with a finger and thumb. "Mistimed it. Was moving slower than I thought. I looked back in the mirror, and he was still standing, leaning against a car, and holding onto some tall cane."

"Was it Robert Anthony's boy? I swear that kid has a death wish. He won't make it to age ten," John Jr said.

"That boy sure can run, can't he?" Walt remarked.

"Most of 'em can. Can't outrun my gun though." Roy pulled his gun from his pants and waved it.

"Wasn't Robert Anthony's boy. This fellow was old. Only got 'bout a few more breaths before he's a goner. I tried to put the old geezer out of his wasted air misery." Walt spat out a hunk of tobacco and swallowed the remaining brown spit. Removing a pack from the pocket of his overalls, he gripped another wad of tobacco and stuffed it in his mouth. Chewing and chawing on it, he tucked it between his cheek and gum. "It's getting late. Ma brought over an apple pie she baked earlier today that smelt up the whole house. Family recipe—"

"Recipe. Yeah, we know, Walt. Been in your family for generations," Roy remarked.

Walt chuckled. "And it's the best apple pie in the world." He crammed the tobacco package back into his pocket. "I still gotta get home. Claire's ovulating. I'm hoping tonight's the night."

"Good luck, Walt." John Jr. patted him on the shoulder and shook it.

"I'll take that. I need all the luck I can get. You know we've been trying for a while." Throwing his head back, Walt drank down the last of the three jars of moonshine from a mason jar he'd clung to.

Not perceiving the effects of the moonshine, he wobbled when he staggered away. "See you, fellows, later."

"Drive safe, Walt." Roy held up his can of beer.

Walt careened to a nearby table where he placed his jar next to others that were set to be used as shooting targets. He shook a few hands and nodded good evening to his cohorts as he tripped his way to his truck, where he dug deep into a pocket in his overalls and pulled out his keys. While backing up his truck, he almost hit the tree behind him before driving off.

Intoxicated from the moonshine and with a loose grip on the steering wheel, he swerved all over the dark grassy tire-tracked path. He flipped the headlights on and off to aid his inebriated vision but failed to elucidate the blurred illusion of his surroundings. The driving path and the tall grass and bushes that surrounded him blended into one. He rubbed and widened his eyes for additional help.

Ahead of him was a familiar narrow wooden suspension bridge that many had missed when crossing late at night. Walt sat up and leaned forward to focus. A thick ghostly fog had collected over the water, making it even harder to see. He flipped on the fog lights. "Is that? That is. That's that nigger. How'd you get all the way out here?" He straightened himself in the seat. "That's alright. I missed you earlier, but I won't miss you tonight. No witnesses, you old geezer."

Shifting gears, Walt grinned and powered down on the pedal. The engine roared and the truck sped up.

The old man turned and looked straight into the vehicle's headlights. No need to run, this time the inevitable was doomed to happen.

Boom. The truck struck the side of the bridge and left the ground, hoisting upward with only air below. With a loud crash, it landed upside down, tires facing up and fast spinning. Black smoke spewed from the damaged engine.

Inside, Walt's contorted body pressed against the door. Moaning, he tried to raise his head, but the pain of a broken bone protruding from his leg brought on shock. He passed out.

Innocent of despicable deeds and aloof to the drowning of an unconscious victim, the once sleeping river was undisturbed by the outstretched arms attached to a body floating face up. The unconscious man's wet boots pointed to the sky, looking newly shined.

On the riverbank, a leather satchel hung from the head of a staff that patiently waited for its owner to awaken, as it had many times before.

Chapter 2

Walt's green eyes scrambled to make sense of his surroundings. A move too fast and, pain counseled him to lay still.

"Awh." He squeezed his eyes tight then slowly opened them to return to his visual excursion.

He was in a small, wooden cabin. A person stood with his back to him.

Learning he wasn't alone in the strange place birthed fear and urgency. "What the... Hey! Hey, what's going on? Where am I? Hey!"

He tried to sit up but found his movement hindered. "What the hell? Hey, why're my hands..." He looked down toward his feet. "...and my foot. Why am I chained to the bed?" All of his clothes had been removed except for his pants.

He tried to move his free leg. "Awh!" The rush of pain from a wrapped broken leg defeated his will.

"Hey, wh...what's this?" He pulled against the bracelets that shackled his wrists and leg. A brief stop and grunt and another pull elevated the pain. He dropped his head back to the bed.

Tension built in his face as anger motivated another attempt to break free regardless of the pain. With a balled fist, Walt grunted. "Uggghhh!" He took a deep breath and repeated. "Uggghhh! Damn, man, what the hell? Arrrgh!" Again, he pulled against the bindings at his wrists, but to no avail.

Walt turned to the person across the room for answers. "Hey! Hey, where am I? What is this place? Uncuff me. C'mon, man, come uncuff..."

He squinted and spoke softly. "What's he doing? Hey! What're you doing over there?"

The man stood before a huge black kettle. Mysteriously unattached to anything, it hung above a fire pit in the floor. With both hands, he stirred a thick liquid with an old wooden spoon half the length of his body.

The man released the spoon to lean against the kettle and slowly walked to a shelf where he gathered four small bottles. He set them on a primitive wooden table near the kettle and one by one, poured modest splashes of liquid from each into the brew before placing each back on the table.

Walt watched curiously. "What's he brewing? I'on know, but um not waiting around to find out." He balled his fist and pulled franticly against the chains. "I have to get the hell out of here."

The restraints that held him hostage limited his view. Frowning, he sniffed the air. "What's that sm—" His nostrils flared and his eyes returned to the huge kettle. "Damn, that stinks."

Blue, green, gray, and charcoal vapors rose from the kettle and filled the air with its appalling smell. The man quietly continued stirring, never taking his eyes from the brew.

The man's silence enraged Walt. "Hey!" Yelling hard, he scratched his dry throat. "Ahem. Hey, nigger! Get over here and unchain me. Ahem. Hey! If you know what's good for you."

The man kept stirring.

"Take these chains off me!" He snatched, yanked, and soared with panic. His eyes traveled faster, looking around the cabin. "There has to be something in here to help me escape this nightmare."

The cabin was old. From the look of the outdated rusty tools that were the home of spider webs hanging on the walls, it was probably built in the pioneer ages. Well-kept vintage bottles of various shapes and sizes and colors sat on shelves, but what caught Walt's eye and made them widen in surprise was the tall staff leaning near the door. "It can't be. What the—"

"I looked back in the mirror, and he was still standing, leaning against a car and holding on to some tall cane," he recalled saying to John Jr. at the barn meeting.

On nearby hooks were a black hat and a long black trench coat. On another hook hung a brown leather satchel. His thoughts went to the conversation he and Roy had while waiting for the traffic light to change.

"What's that on his shoulder?"

"Looks like a satchel. Like an old worn leather satchel. He's ancient."

Walt's eyes raced back to the man whose back was still to him. "You're that nigger. That old geezer I tried to run over. Twice! Hey! Hey!"

The old man didn't turn from the substance in the kettle. He placed a large dipper that was hanging on a nearby wall into the brew. Lifting it from the brew, he tilted the dipper forward, spilling it back into the pot to check the thickness.

"Hey...hey, old man. Hey, let me go." He didn't receive any response. "Hey, man, come let me loose. I won't hurt you."

Resting the dipper in the brew, the old man took two of the small bottles from the table and poured another draught from each. He returned them to the table, grabbed onto the ladle with both hands, and stirred.

Behind him, Walt pulled against the chains with all his might. "Uggghhh! Damn! Hey! Hey, man, come let me loose. You got no right holding me here against my will. The law will come after you if you hurt me. Hey!" Balling his fists, he tried to snatch loose. "Hrrr! HEY! Let me loose, man! Unloose me from these damn chains!"

Ignoring Walt, the man took an antique white tin cup with blue trim from the table. He scooped the thick liquid with the dipper and poured it into the cup, filling it to the rim. Turning in Walt's direction, he slowly crept across the wooden floor and stopped next to his bed. He tucked a hand beneath Walt's head, lifted it, and put the cup to his mouth.

Walt tightened his lips and shook his head right and left in refusal.

The old man gestured for him to drink by moving the cup closer to his mouth.

"Get that away from my mouth if you know what's good for you."

The old man put the cup closer to Walt's mouth and signaled with a nod of his head for Walt to drink.

Walt turned away.

He signaled again with a slight raise of the cup.

"No, you old fuck!"

The old man forced Walt's head further forward to assure he'd see what was to come. He hovered the cup over Walt's waist and tilted. Thick, steaming fluid slithered over the rim and smack onto Walt's stomach.

In anguish, Walt let out a gut-wrenching squeal that quickly turned into a throaty growl. Thick chunks of what looked like regurgitated pineapples, bananas and raisins mixed with slimy oily oatmeal lay burning his skin, passing through the first layer, and baking into the second, then the third.

"Arrrgggh!" Walt balled in his lips. His chest pumped up and down as he took in quick racing breaths to bear the burning sensation. His beige face turned burgundy.

The old man brought the tin cup back to Walt's face and tilted it, allowing him to see that it was completely empty.

Walt's eyes grew heavy as the substance burned through his stomach and bubbled up. Steam rose like the vapors from the boiling pot. Walt let out a loud howling cry. His eyes rolled back and closed.

Chapter 3

"You up now? Hey, are you awake?"

A slightly French accent filled the room. A woman dipped a woven nylon cloth into a basin filled with cold water and squeezed. With its dampness, she patted Walt's face in several places as his eyes fought to open. Removing the cloth from his forehead, she dipped it into the water again, squeezed, and patted his forehead and face. She repeated the questions several times before Walt was finally able to open his eyes to confront the beautiful tan-skinned woman with long straight black hair hanging down her back. She had full lips and a beauty mark in the form of a mole that rested on the side of her left nostril and looked like a nose piercing. Freckles danced from one side of her cheek to the other.

"Wh-where am I?" Walt looked around the room. "This ain't the same place."

"Shhh. Just rest. All your answers will come later." Her small feminine hand pressed the moist cloth against his forehead.

"Am I dreaming again?" Turning his head from side to side, his weary eyes struggled to remain open. "Where's the old man? It was a dream. It must've been a dream."

When the woman turned to dip the cloth again, Walt tried to raise his head to see his stomach. She put fingers to his forehead and gently pressed his head back to the bed. "No-no...you need to rest."

"But—"

"Rest now. It's too soon to get up. Your leg isn't well enough."

"My leg," he remembered. "The truck...the accident. The pain. I must be in a hospital. I must've been in a coma or dreaming." He looked around the room. "What's this? Where's this place? Is this a cabin? Am I still in the cabin?"

There were three cots in the room. He laid on one.

"You've been here for two weeks."

"Been here? Where's here—where am I?"

"On Ms. Lora Dean's Plantation."

"Lora Dean...plantation? What's this, some kind of camp?"

"Camp?" She laughed. "No, this isn't a camp. It's a plantation. Owned by Ms. Lora Dean."

"How did I get here?"

"Your master sold you to her."

"*My master?* What the f—"

"Just rest. You need to rest, so you can heal. Ms. Lora Dean wants you up and working. That means it's up to me—I'm Paty, by the way—to get you well enough, so you can work. And that means I need to get that fever out of you."

Walt looked around the shack again. The pain in his leg limited every motion. He threw his head back. "This has to be a dream. I can't be living this. Plantation. Sold. *Master*." He shook his head. "Up and working!" With widened eyes, his hand rushed to his stomach.

Paty looked at him. "Yeah, it was pretty bad when you first got here. They said one of those dogs took a chunk out of your stomach and ate at it like it was food. It's gonna leave a bad scar, but it won't be long before it's all healed up. And your leg too. You're going to walk again, but with a limp." She giggled. "Limp or not, I have to get you out of this bed, so you can get to work. Especially a strong, dark man like you."

"What did you say?" Walt raised a hand and stopped it in mid-air. He stared at it dumbfounded then found his voice and said with speed, "No, no, no, no, no, no, no, no, no, no." He brought up the other hand, rotated them both from front to back, then rushed them to his hair. "It can't be. This can't be."

"You talk funny," she said about his southern country accent. She walked to a table.

Ignoring her, he continued rubbing his hair. The texture was an overload of truth. "Um having a dream. I must be—"

"No, sir, this isn't a dream. You're here with me in the sickhouse?"

"*Sickhouse?*" Walt's eyes rolled back and closed. He lay still and sensed his body for pain, trying his best to feel it. Trying to— "I'd rather be dead." He lay still for a few minutes. "Lord, wake me up from this unrealistic dream." After a while, his eyes swung open. He rose.

Paty rushed back over, and with a palm to his chest, pushed him to the bed. "Uh-uh. You have to be still. You're still healing. When Ms. Lora Dean learns you're awake, she'll wanna have a look at you. See for herself."

Walt shook his head over and over. *It has to be a dream; it has to be. It ain't real.* His left arm went across his forehead. When he opened his eyes again, he stopped at the sight of the shack's ceiling. Dark yellowed dried mud sealed the beams. "What year is this?"

"Year? 1815."

"18...15?"

"Yes."

"And this is a plantation?"

"Yes."

"Are you...a slave?"

She grinned. "All my life."

"What about me? Am I...ah...?"

The twenty-eight-year-old smiled. "You're Black, aren't you?" Paty had been raised by a French doctor and was well versed in proper grammar. She looked at Walt. "Black folks are slaves. It's always been that way."

"Black? Like a nigger? Are you sure?"

"You saw your hands and felt the hair on your head. What do you think? White folks' hair doesn't feel like that. You're Black. Are you feeling alright?" She touched his forehead. "Fever's gone down some."

"How did I get here?"

"I told you. Your master sold you to Ms. Lor—"

"No, I mean...how did I get here? In this time period?"

"Oh, you mean why were you sold to Ms. Lora Dean. They said you ran...but that the dogs caught you. They broke one of your legs and cut off one of your toes, so you can't run anymore. Then they sold you to Ms. Lora Dean. They brought you to me like they do all the broken slaves. For me to put you back together again. What does that tell you? They don't do that to White folks."

"But I am White."

"White, huh?" She touched his forehead. "It has to be the fever talking."

Chapter 4

The door swung open and in trampled a plump tall White woman with a long oval-shaped face. Her brunette hair was pulled up into a bun. She was the widow of Old Massa Herman, a man twice her age. He had died a day shy of his sixty-ninth birthday a couple of years back.

At the age of thirty-six, twelve years after her belated husband had asked her father for his only daughter's hand in marriage, Lora Dean became the sole owner of her late husband's small plantation. A clinical practice for badly injured and sick slaves.

Years prior, Lora Dean lived with her parents. They had no wealthy name to help push their only child over the matrimony threshold. When she met Herman, she didn't want to marry him.

"Do you want to be married?" her mother asked her daughter.

"Yes, but not to a tiny old man."

"Who says you'll get another chance. You're twenty-four, and the only interest you ever had was from that boy. None from our kind. You've been soiled, Lora Dean."

Lora Dean dropped her head.

"And soon, your childbearing years will be gone. With him, we know you'll be taken care of."

"If I have a choice between being lonely for the rest of my life and marrying an old man, I would rather be lonely."

"And what happens after me and your papa die? All we have is this house. How will you survive?"

"I'll get a job."

"Doing what? Everyone who can afford to pay has slaves."

"I can teach."

"You said you hated school. Me and your papa made a great sacrifice to send you to that school for teaching. You were gone but a few months and got thrown out. Came back with that big mistake in tow. And you spread wider after that."

"Mama, I know what happened to me. I'd rather not be reminded."

"Well, schooling is out. We don't have any more money."

"What about the money you made from the sale of my big mistake in tow?"

"Don't sass me, child."

Lora Dean dropped her head. "Yes, ma'am."

"Besides, we didn't make any money. We made a trade for this house. It ain't much, but it's all we have. Your papa assured a roof over mine and your head after he's dead and gone."

"So, I paid for it with my mistake."

"Lora Dean, it was the best thing for you. For us. Maybe just...just give this a chance. See what happens."

"Mama, I don't wanna marry that old man. How old is he anyway?"

Lowering her head, Mary swallowed deeply. "It shouldn't matter. You give him an heir, he'll give you a good life. That's a fair trade."

Twelve years later, Herman looked his wife in the face as she stood over his dying bed. "You're barren, Lora Dean. You couldn't give me an heir. You've been a good wife, but kindness doesn't take the place of an heir to leave my fortune to."

Herman died heartbroken, disappointed, and resentful of the woman he'd placed all his paternal hopes in.

Chapter 5

As the sole proprietor of the plantation, Lora Dean entered the sickhouse. She stopped at the foot of Walt's bed. Her eyes were fast upon him. "I have word that he's recuperating. Is that true, Paty?"

"Yes, ma'am, he's doing much better."

Walt returned Lora Dean's stare.

"Are your eyes on me, boy?"

Confused and still hoping he was dreaming; he had no idea how to respond. He continued staring.

"Hmp." She walked to the head of his bed and smacked him.

Walt's hand rushed to the side of his face. Shock demanded he keep staring.

"You mind your eyes, boy! I see why he was sold so cheap. Not only is he damaged physically, he has no manners. We'll have to teach him the Lora Dean's way. One week. Get him well so we can get him to the field. One of our mules just died. I need a hauler."

"Yes, ma'am."

Lora Dean looked at Walt, who dropped his head after quickly learning not to stare at a White woman. She stomped out of the cabin.

Paty went to Walt's bedside carrying a small wooden bowl of food and a spoon and sat down next to him to ladle the food into his mouth. "You better mind your place. I don't know how they did it on the plantation where you came from, but Ms. Lora Dean, she doesn't take kindly to slaves looking at White folks. Come on, let's get you better. Sit up so you can eat."

Walt was still angry from the slap, and his sullen face showed it.

"It's not worth being mad. Anger doesn't help any. It only makes it worse."

The door flew open. They both looked toward it.

"Oh, I've decided on his name. He'll be called Tondey."

"Tondey, ma'am?" Paty questioned.

"Yes, Tondey."

"Oh, hell no."

Ms. Lora Dean walked up to him. "What did you say, boy?"

"Ain't no way um answering to no nigger name. My name's Walt."

With fiery eyes, Ms. Lora Dean grabbed a nearby stick that Paty used for splints. With all her might, she slapped him upside the head, breaking the splint in two and knocking Walt halfway out of the bed. Throwing the broken stick to the floor, she looked at Paty. "Get him well enough for the field. Knot on his head or not, he's going to the field in a week."

"Yes, ma'am." Paty stood frozen. As soon as Ms. Lora Dean left, she rushed over to pull Walt back into the bed and went for a moist cloth.

Walt sat up with tears in his eyes. When he rubbed them away, the old man from the bridge was standing in the corner of the room.

Paty brought over a damp cloth and laid it on his cut temple.

The pain from the moist cloth against the swelling cut was sharp. Walt jumped and looked at her.

"It's alright. I'm just laying this on that knot that's coming."

He turned back to the old man. "It's that old man. The one who put me here. You get me out of here, old man, or I'll kill you."

"Who are you talking to, Tondey?"

Walt looked at Paty, then turned back to the corner of the room. "My name's Walt. And um talking to that old man. The one I tried to run over. See 'im. See 'im over there." He pointed.

Paty turned in the direction of his finger and giggled. "That hit to your head has you seeing things."

He dropped his hand. "Maybe I am." He looked in the corner again. The old man was still there.

Putting the cloth on the table, she grabbed the bowl and spoon. "Come on, eat up." She raised the bowl of food toward his face.

He turned to her, then to the old man, and back to her when she spoke.

"You can't test Ms. Lora Dean like that. You must learn the ways of this plantation. You know what? You need to be up in a week. Might as well start now. Here..." She put the bowl of food and spoon in his hands. "Go on, eat. In one week, you have to be out of this bed and in the field. Like Ms. Lora Dean said, knot or not."

Chapter 6

No matter the rushed time she'd given him, Lora Dean was no fool. She purchased slaves to make them better and she knew the week she'd given for Walt to heal was not enough. However, as soon as she got word that he had fully recovered, she told Paty, "Get him up and out in the field."

"Tondey, let me take a look at you." Standing next to his bed, Paty bent over and examined Walt's stomach, then his leg. "Yeah, that looks good...and that too. All better. Let me see your head."

He hesitated and was angered that she'd called him Tondey.

"Come on let me see," she said.

He leaned his head toward her.

"Yep, you're all better. Can't even tell that your head met with my favorite splint. It's time for you to leave the sickhouse, Tondey."

"I told you my name ain't no blasted Tondey."

"Then, what is it?"

"Walt."

"Is that the name Ms. Lora Dean gave you?"

"My mama named me Walt. It's the only name I've ever answered to."

"Where's your mama now?"

"She's—she's back in—"

"It doesn't matter where she is. On this plantation, Ms. Lora Dean is the mother of us all. And she names all her children, except for me. My name has always been Paty. It came from my first master."

"Um not her child. She didn't labor and birth me. Only that earns the right to name me."

"That may be, but Ms. Lora Dean doesn't have any children. She's barren. So, we're her children. She names us, and that way we're hers. And she gave you the name Tondey. It's who you are and what I'll keep calling you. Now, come on, get out of this bed, Tondey."

"This can't be real."

"What can't be real? Your name?"

"You, this shack, me. That old man standing over there who keeps looking at me." His southern country dialect was constantly fading the more he spoke.

"Old man this. Old man that. There is no one is in this room but you and me."

Walt turned to the old man in the corner of the room. "Yeah, well, he's there." He turned to Paty. Intensity filled his face as if he needed her to hear and believe him. "You listen to me. I'm a White man. My name's Walt, not Tondey. And that nigger over there done put me here with that stuff he poured on my stomach. He put some kind've—some kind've hex of me." He pointed to his chest with a single finger. "Um a White man—"

"You're a White man? Ha! And the rest of us Black folks are niggers." She reached for the handheld reflector and shoved it in his face. "Is that a White man staring back at you? You're darker than Black Bean Ray, and he's the darkest slave on this plantation. You're the darkest I've ever seen. Look at your arm. You're Black. And no matter what name your mother gave you, your new name is Tondey. The name Ms. Lora Dean gave you. You're a Black slave named Tondey, and this is real. Like it or not, it's all real. Except for your old man in the corner. He's not real. And we, the slaves, will call you Tondey. Those White folks are going to call you nigger. Just like you're referring to that invisible man in the corner." She turned to the corner. "There's no one over there. Just my splints hanging on the wall, Tondey."

"Um Walt."

Chapter 7

The very next day, Walt stepped into the glaring daylight. It was his first day outside facing the new world he'd found himself in.

"Is this him?" the hog and cattle keeper asked Paty who was standing in the doorway of the sickhouse waiting for him to come get Walt.

"Yeah, he's all fixed up for you, Rudy."

"C'mon," Rudy said. "We have to get these hogs fed."

Walt followed him.

"We ain't like other plantations who buy slaves to work what they sell. Our master sells warm bodies. On this plantation, we eat what we grow. We sell meat sometimes too, at the market, but our meat be mostly for the kitchen and the storage house for us and Ms. Lora Dean. She allows us to eat good too.

"There ain't but three of us to tend to the hogs and cattle. You make four. Yeah, I can count a little. Up to ten, I can count. Come on. We have a lotta work to do with only a few hands to do it. Let's get to it. Stopping to get you done slowed me down. We gotta make up for that time."

Limping behind Rudy, Walt looked back at Paty still standing in the doorway. He collided into the back of Rudy.

"Hey, watch your step. You'll get to the field soon enough."

"Um sorry, man."

"What you go by?"

"Walt."

Still within earshot, Paty yelled, "Not anymore. Ms. Lora Dean named him Tondey."

Walt scowled at the woman who had nursed him back to health. *Now she's throwing me to the wolves.*

"If Ms. Lora Dean says it Tondey, then that's what it is. C'mon, Tondey. Let's get to work."

"My name's Walt."

Rudy stopped and turned to him. "Let's get this here straight. Whatever name Ms. Lora Dean done gave you, that's what um calling you. What did she say to call you?"

Walt didn't answer.

Paty chimed in, "She said his name—"

"At!" Rudy raised his hand. "Naw, let him say."

Walt stood tall, sticking out his chest.

"Hey, we have a lotta work to do, and I ain't got no time to be fooling up with you. Now, you're gonna tell me your name, or you'll get strung up."

"By who? You?"

As tall as Walt was, Rudy loomed over him. The older, muscular Rudy took a step closer to Walt and looked down directly into his eyes. "Don't test me. I don't fool around with fools."

Walt could see that the crazed look Rudy held was no daring matter. Turning away from Rudy, his eyes beheld the small plantation. He took inventory of all his eyes could see. *Am I the only White man on this plantation?*

"Hey, you plan to tell me your name? It's the last time um gonna ask."

"Tondey." He was still looking over the plantation. "She gave me the name Tondey, but..."

"But what? She gave you that name, that's all there is to it. Nothing else that's in your head matters. Now, let's go get these hogs round up to feed."

Tondey continued taking in the surroundings while he followed Rudy. Rows of dogwood trees flowing pink with flowers made a path to a two-story wooden house with a covered porch. Not far from that was a large standalone building. *What's that used for?*

He stuck out his hands and rotated them from front to back in hopes of finding some sort of doubt that he was witnessing some figment of his imagination. "This ain't no dream. That old nigger geezer hexed me and somehow got me here and gave me this black skin. I'm gonna kill 'im first chance I get."

"Say, what? What's that you're saying?" Rudy said over his shoulder as he continued on the path.

"Nothing." Tondey continued following.

"What did you do on the plantation you came from?"

"I, ah'... I picked cotton?"

"Cotton picking is easy compared to hog raising. We're about to get dirty."

Chapter 8

Following the lead of the other men, Tondey rinsed up after his first day of tending to the cattle and hogs. Right after, he went to the sickhouse and found the clothes he'd been sleeping in had been washed and neatly folded on the bed.

Paty nodded at them. "Those are your clothes. You have on the set for the field. Then that set is for after you leave the field." She laid the things she was holding on top of the folded clothes. "Here's a string for your pants, a pair of shoes when you're not in the field, and a few other things, like a blanket for your bed. Mawbee has your bed ready. It's not much, I know, but Ms. Lora Dean, she tries to be better than most massas."

Black Bean Ray, who was the darkest slave on the plantation before Tondey came, walked into the sickhouse. "You ready?" he asked Tondey.

"Ready for what?"

"You'll be in the shack with me. C'mon, get your things and let's go."

Tondey huffed.

"C'mon, man, get to it. Um hungry. Sup should be ready."

"Why do I have to move out of here?" Tondey looked at Paty.

Black Bean Ray scoffed. "'Cause this is the sickhouse. You might work like you're sick, but you don't need to be here. Now, get your stuff and let's go."

Tondey snatched up his things from the bed.

"Are you taking him around to see the plantation?" Paty asked.

"You ain't showed him yet?"

She pointed. "You see them two sick slaves in those beds? That's what I do. That's my job on this plantation. And I have one more coming two days from now. Ms. Lora Dean wants them up and out in a month's time. I don't have time to show him around."

"C'mon!" Black Bean Ray waved for Tondey to follow him. "I'll show you around. First, we gotta drop off your things."

Walking beside Tondey, Black Bean Ray pointed ahead. "That right there's where we live. I used to share it with another slave, but even Paty wasn't able to save 'im after that horse plowed 'im in the chest."

"Paty's like the miracle worker around here, huh?"

"Ain't too many slaves she's lost. I seen her bring a few back from the dead."

Hugging his items to his chest, Tondey looked at Black Bean Ray. "From the dead. You're exaggerating a bit much, don't you think?"

"What's that you said? Air-ga-tatin'.."

"Exaggerating...making a story sounds bigger than it is."

"Exag—"

"Niggers are a bunch of dumb ff—" he mumbled. "Never mind."

"No, sir. A year ago, she snatched a couple of them from death. By the time those slaves got here, they were damn near dead. Burning up with fever. We thought for sure, they weren't gonna make it. A month later, they were up and walking and sold to the massa with the most money."

"Where'd she learn to heal people? She some kind've voodoo doctor?"

"Voodoo, no, sir. Paty, she's special. She was raised by a doctor from France after her ma died. Her ma used to help the doctor treat patients. Some say Paty might be his child with her having White in her. And she got that long black silky hair that reaches down her back.

"The doctor fell in love with an American woman and followed her back to the states. He brought Paty with 'im. It's said he never let her outta his sight. Where he went, she went. He taught her everything he knew. When he died, his wife sold her.

"Ms. Lora Dean, she learned of Paty after the doctor visited her sick husband way before he died. When she heard that the doctor was dead, she rushed out and bought her for her sick slaves. Paid a lot of money for her too."

"Smart lady. How old is she?"

"Who, Paty or Ms. Lora Dean?"

"Paty."

Black Bean Ray stopped in front of the shack. "Oh, no, you don't. Don't go getting no thinking in your head about getting with Paty. She's off-limits. No husband, no children. That's the way Ms. Lora Dean wants it."

"I wasn't—"

"Here it is." Black Bean Ray opened the door and pointed. "Gone, put your stuff on the bed on that side."

Tondey looked around the tiny one-room shack that had two beds, one door, and a hole in the wall used as a window. A few pieces of garments were thrown on the floor at the foot of Black Bean Ray's bed.

"It stinks in here." Tondey walked in, dropped his things on the bed, and returned outside.

"That's working man's scent. I gotta get my things washed." Black Bean Ray closed the door behind them and pointed as they walked away. "You see these shacks along this here path?"

Tondey looked.

"It's where we, the slaves live."

"How many slaves do y'all have on this plantation?"

"You mean how many slaves *we have*? You're a part of us now 'til Ms. Lora Dean decides to sell you. Let's see. We have me, you, Wink, and Rudy who work the barn, hogs, and cattle. Then there's Lillie, who grows the vegetables. Ms. Lora Dean named her Lillie 'cause she works with the plants.

"Boon and Laudee, they work in the kitchen." He leaned near Tondey. "They're husband and wife, but Ms. Lora don't know. Secret marriage. Then there're Mawbee and Adessa in the big house who cares for Mrs. Lora Dean and the house. Adessa, she does the washing too. She washes for all of us. Lillie lives in the big house with them too. And there's Paty.

"All of us came to Ms. Lora Dean and her husband sick or hurt, accept Mawbee and Paty. We got well on this plantation. Now, we're Ms. Lora Dean's property since her husband is dead."

"That's nine of you. Ten if you count me."

Black Bean Ray stopped and turned to Tondey. "Boy, you can count?"

"Yeah." He grinned proudly.

"Let that be your secret. Ms. Lora Dean learns of it, and you'll be in a heap of trouble. Now, you know that's where the barn is. Over there is the wash pump where we clean up after work and that's the well." The tour ended with them standing in front of the large building Tondey had wondered about earlier. "This here is the sup house."

"Sup house?"

"Yeah, it's where the food's cooked and the slaves eat. Except the house slaves. They have a room in the big house where they eat and live. Ms. Lora Dean tries to keep them away from us. So they can't tend to gossip."

"How can I get a job in the big house?"

"Ha! You'll be lucky if you carry water to the big house."

Tondey looked at his hands. "Oh, yeah, um too dark."

"Yep, that's it." Black Bean Ray opened the door with a big grin. "Mmm, you smell that cooking?"

"Hurry up and shut that door! Flies coming in." Boon sat a stack of plates on a table. "Who you got there, Black Bean Ray? That the new slave who the dog had for sup?"

All the slaves who'd gathered in the supper house, Rudy, Wink, Lillie, Laudee, Black Bean Ray, and Boon had a good laugh.

Tondey frowned. *Bunch of black smut clowns. Ain't nothing funny. I'll make you regret it.*

Chapter 9

In his former life, Walt was employed as a line lead at a chicken plant where he stood around giving orders. No hard, physical labor for him; he labored others. Now a slave, Tondey found himself on the opposite side of the employment line. He was being slaved while taking orders from a slave.

His working days were long and the labor taxing. He noticed the difference on his first day of physical labor. After work and supper, with little strength left, Tondey crawled onto a wooden lumpy partition that was his bed to get much-needed rest. "Whoa! What the hell is this thing made of?"

"Wood, some old rags, and straw." Black Bean Ray sat and took off his shoes.

"It's nothing like the bed in the sickhouse."

"That's because those beds are meant to help you heal."

"Well, this one will send you to the sickhouse."

That night, Tondey tossed and turned. Taking the blanket Paty had packed for him, he balled it up and tucked it beneath his head. "It's hot as hell in here!"

"You're lucky. The last plantation I was on, it was about seven of us in one small shack. There was dirt for the floors. It was one big wooden hot box with cracks in the walls that bugs crawled in. The roof leaked rain, babies crying. All the stench of the cotton fields in one small, crowded room. This room is tight, but it's just us. It's hot, but we don't have to share the air with nobody but us. Our beds may not be like the ones in the sickhouse, but at least they're not the floor. I've learned to appreciate what I have. Could be worse. Could always be worse."

Lying on his side, sweat fell from Tondey's temple onto the bed. "I can't imagine it being worse than this." As the night grew cooler, Tondey fell asleep until a bug bit his leg. He sprung up. "Hmp. What do you want?" He gawked at the quiet old man across from him. "You get me back home this second."

Black Bean Ray woke up. "Who you talking to?"

"That old geezer. You don't see 'im?"

"See who?"

"The old—"

"Get some sleep. Work coming soon enough. No need for us to rush it." Black Bean Ray rolled onto his side and faced the wall. Not long after, he was sound asleep.

With the old man still in view, Tondey lay back down and slipped his arms underneath his head.

A loud sound came from Black Bean Ray.

"Whew, you stink." Tondey fanned his nose.

The old man stood silently, his eyes never leaving Tondey.

"What do you want from me? Tell me?" He stared back. "Tell me, old man."

After a while of staring with no response, Tondey's eyes grew heavy. Sleep followed.

~~~~~

On a late afternoon, the sun displayed its greatest talents with glowing rays and perfect hot heat. Beneath it all, Tondey chased hogs with loud, aggressive hollers, unlike his usual self. "Yaw, yaw! Get! Get your hog asses back in there!"

Rudy walked near Black Bean Ray. "What's wrong with Lazy Dazy over there?"

"Talking about Tondey? I don't know. Something's wrong. He ain't never worked like this before."

"Probably need a woman."

They laughed. Rudy gave Black Beans Ray's shoulder a soft pound and they resumed work.

"Hhh, hah!" Tondey continued.

Several hogs broke free and raced toward the barn's exit, getting Rudy's attention. "Tondey! Get them hogs back in the pen."

"Um trying. They..." Tondey tried to redirect the hogs back into the pen, but slipped. Flopping on his stomach, mud splattered and smacked him in the face.

Rudy, Black Bean Ray, and Wink laughed.

Tondey tried to get up but fell again. He was completely covered in mud. Making it to a sitting position, he slapped the mud, then sputtered when it flew up into his eyes. "You nasty hogs! Mud sucking hogs!"

The other men slapped their legs as Tondey sat looking disgusted and mud quickly dried on his face until Rudy barked, "Go help that fool get up."

Black Bean Ray and Wink ran over to Tondey and then everyone got back to work.

Chapter 10

Easing out of bed, Adessa tipped-toed toward the door.

A whisper in the dark room came from the top of the hierarchy of slaves. "Ms. Lora Dean finds out, you're gonna be sold like all the other women Black Bean Ray slept with."

"Oh, hush, Mawbee. Who's gonna tell her—you?"

"In this room, no talk gets out, but out of this room, talk gets in."

"Ms. Lora Dean gets hers, don't she? I want mine too."

Mawbee slipped from beneath the covers, lit the lantern and stood. "What do you mean, Ms. Lora Dean gets hers?"

"I ain't saying."

"You've already said. Finish it."

Adessa shrugged her shoulder.

"Child, say it, or I'll tell Ms. Lora Dean where you go late at night."

Sticking out her lips, Adessa looked at Mawbee. "I thought you said no talk gets out of this room."

"Say it, girl. What do you know that I don't?"

Adessa relaxed her shoulders and smiled slightly. "Ms. Lora Dean, she's expecting."

Mawbee frowned. The shocking news turned up her curiosity to its highest level of intensity. Her voice raised to a high pitch. "Expecting? What do you mean? She's expecting company?"

"She's expecting company alright, but not the kind you're thinking about."

Mawbee walked over to the door and pulled on the knob to make sure it was closed tightly. She looked back at Lillie who was sound asleep, then returned to Adessa. "What are you saying?"

Adessa sighed. "I wash Ms. Lora Dean's clothes, and I ain't seen no red stains in months."

"How many?"

"Two, at least."

"So...some women skip. It's always been that way."

"Uh-uh, not Ms. Lora Dean. She's a heavy leaker. She stains her sheets and bottoms every time, and she ain't stained either in a while."

"But who? How? Her husband's been dead for years. He said she was barren."

"From what I heard that old fool was too old to make a baby. Maybe he was the barren one. In sixty-nine years, he ain't got no woman pregnant."

"We don't know that. Maybe there's a bastard child somewhere."

"Maybe there is, maybe there ain't. It don't matter. He ain't leave no bun in her belly all these years since he's been dead."

"Who would be the dadd..." Mawbee thought.

"Overseer comes when beckoned. Maybe it's his. She left for a social a few times. Maybe she met a man."

Mawbee's eyes widened. "That's it. That's it. She met somebody. Maybe she's getting married."

"Or..."

"Or what?" Mawbee gave a curious stare.

"Maybe, just maybe..."

"Say it, girl!"

"Maybe she's been with one of these slaves."

Whack! Mawbee's hand went across Adessa's face, leaving a handprint on her peach skin. "You watch your mouth. Slaves be hung for staring at White folks, much less sleeping with a White woman. Every man on this plantation knows that. Word gets back in town that Ms. Lora Dean's been with a slave and one of our good slave men will die for sure. All 'em if no one tells who the father is. And Ms. Lora Dean will be the talk of the town. Her good name gone to pieces."

Holding her face, Adessa looked at Lillie who'd awakened. She walked toward the door and looked back at Mawbee. "Somebody's the daddy. And in some months, we're gonna see who end up dead. Her good name or our good slave men." She tightened her lips and rushed off barefooted.

Adessa tapped lightly on a shack's door and it eased open. A hand reached out and pulled her inside. She immediately wrapped her arms around Black Bean Ray's neck and rested the side of her face on his chest. She hugged him tightly.

"Hey, hey, you almost choking me." He pulled her arms from his neck. "What's the matter? Are you alright?"

Kissing his neck and cheek, she stepped back and slipped her thin dress over her head. She had no clothes beneath it. Reaching for his pants, she untied them. They fell to the floor. Backing up to his bed, Adessa sat, reached, and grabbed his thick, long fingers, and pulled him toward her. As she climbed further into the bed, she lured him on top of her.

The pleasing sounds of sexual pleasure awakened Tondey, who lay quietly, taking in what the darkness did not allow him to see. Finally, the slapping of bodies stopped and was replaced by conversation that kept Tondey awake and listening.

"What's the matter, Dessa? What's wrong?"

She gave up the warmth of his chest on her back and turned toward him. "I hear I ain't the only woman who's been in your bed."

He rolled onto his back in the narrow bed and slipped an arm beneath his head. "That's why you're upset. Hm? ... Yeah, it's true. I've had other women in my bed, but not at the same time. Every woman I loved—Ms. Lora Dean takes 'em away. You know she don't allow no relationships on her plantation. She figured since her husband's dead and she ain't got no man, no other woman on her plantation can have a man. And if there's no husband, there's no loving. No loving, no children. This plantation is barren like her. I ain't seen a child since I was a child, and that was on another plantation."

"Well, that's gonna change soon."

He turned to face her. "What? What are you saying, girl? You're preg—? You can't be...you-you can't—Mrs. Lora Dean will sell you for sure if she finds out." He jumped out of bed and hurriedly slipped on his pants."

"What are you doing?"

Breathing hard, Black Bean Ray scrambled in the dark to locate his shirt. He found a piece of garment on the floor and threw it to her. "I think that's yours. Put it on. We gotta run. I can't let her sell you like she sold the other women from me." He scrambled around the foot of his bed, searching for his shirt.

"Black Bean?"

"I can't let her sell my woman."

"Black Bean Ray?"

He stopped. His hands went to his hips. Dropping his head, he panted. "I can't...I can't let her sell you, Dessa, I can't. I can't let her sell my woman and my unborn child. Not you too, I won't."

Adessa stood. Wrapping her arms around him from behind, she whispered in his ear. "She ain't gonna sell me 'cause I ain't with child." She kissed his back.

He let out a long trembling sigh. Leaving her arms, he sat on his bed and snatched her beside him. "Then what's this you're talking about?"

She rested the side of her face on his arm. "She's gonna have a baby."

"Who?"

"Ms. Lora Dean. She's pregnant."

~~~~~

The pregnancy news was ignorant of what was to come but liberated enough to know that it wanted all to know of its business. In a hurry to be shared with all gossipers, it made its way to the kitchen.

"Is it true, Mawbee?" Boon asked the moment she walked into the kitchen.

Mawbee ignored him. "Is Ms. Lora Dean's food ready? It's morning. She'll be up shortly." Mawbee moved around the kitchen, looking for the platter specifically used for Ms. Lora Dean's morning meals. She didn't find it. "Boon, I need Ms. Lora Dean's morning platter."

"It's over there. I'll get it." He went for it.

Mawbee waited. "Laudee, how much longer before the food's ready?"

"You can take it now. Hand me her plate, Boon." Laudee reached out, waiting to take the plate.

Boon, Laudee's husband, walked across the large wooden kitchen floor as if he knew every board that crept and handed the plate to Laudee. "Mawbee, you hear what I asked you?"

"Yeah, I heard you, Boon. Your question ain't nothing but gossip. I ain't got no time for no gossip."

"We have a right to know. If there's a baby in the house, we gotta feed it." Boon handed Laudee the lid to the platter.

Laudee finished dressing Ms. Lora Dean's morning meal and topped off the platter with the lid. She walked it over to Mawbee. "Here you go."

Mawbee grasped the platter but was met with resistance when Laudee didn't let go. She looked into Laudee's staring eyes. "Um not sure if she's with child or not, Laudee. When I know for sure, you'll know."

Laudee released the platter and stepped aside, allowing Mawbee to pass. She looked at her husband. "Boon, keep that gossip in this kitchen. When it's time for us to know, Mawbee will tell us."

Chapter 11

"Hey! Hey, Tondey! Tondey! That boy can't hear worth nothing!" Rudy shook his head.

"He can hear. Just don't like that name Ms. Lora Dean done gave 'im," Wink responded.

"I'on blame 'im. That's an ugly name." Black Bean Ray walked up.

They laughed and went back to work.

When the day's work ended, Tondey stormed off the field.

"What's wrong with him?" Wink asked.

"I'on know, but we got more work out of him today than most." Rudy hung his tool. "Let's get out of this field."

After pumping water from the well into a bowl, Tondey angrily walked toward his shack. Water from the shallow container splattered on the ground, leaving only a little to wash away the mud from his clothes and body. He poured the rest over his head and threw the bowl on the ground. Once changed into his one set of clean clothes, he flopped onto the bed.

Black Bean Ray opened the door but stood on the outside. "You coming for sup?"

"Yeah."

Entering the kitchen, Tondey looked around the room and spotted a lonely seat in the back. After getting his food, he ate and filled his mind with the conversation in the room while he made private plans to get back home. *No matter what it cost them.*

Lillie, the garden girl commented on the ongoing rumor while taking her plate of food from Laudee. "I ain't seen no man in her room or in her bed since her husband died in it."

Mawbee walked into the kitchen.

"Lillie!" Mawbee leveled a chastising gaze at the girl.

With her plate in front of her, Lillie dropped her head and rushed out of the kitchen.

As soon as Mawbee got her food and left, the conversation resumed.

"I bet it's the overseer." Boon said. "He stayed late in her study one night. I saw when he left. Came creeping out like he stole something."

"He stole something, alright." Rudy laughed. The others in the room joined him.

"I'on know. I think maybe it's somebody she met when she left." Wink sat with his plate of food. "Some stranger." He scooped up a spoonful and put it in his mouth.

"What about you, Wink? She let you in the house one evening. What she needed you for?" Boon asked.

"You know." Rudy laughed.

"Naw...I moved something heavy for her."

"Well, she is a heavy woman." Rudy joined them at the table with his plate.

They all laughed again.

"Naw...wasn't me. I ain't the pa."

"Well, somebody is." Boon took his plate to Laudee to be filled.

"How do we know for sure that she's with child, Boon? Mawbee ain't said yet," Laudee scorned her husband.

"But Adessa said so, and she washes her clothes. What did you say she said, Black Bean Ray? It's been two months since she's bled?" Rudy asked.

"I ain't say nothing. I'on know how y'all know." He stuffed his mouth with cornbread.

Wink turned around and nodded toward Tondey. "He said."

Chapter 12

In the pitch dark, he listened but kept waiting in the deathly silence. Unable to tell how much time had passed, the drone of steady snoring relieved the fever of his curiosity. "It's time. He's asleep. Finally." Slowly rising from the bed, Tondey crept out of the shack, looked around, and rushed across the lawn, headed for the big house.

He opened the door that was never locked and planted a solid bare foot inside. The other foot followed as he closed the door behind him and turned to find his way. The house was a dark and unfamiliar maze. *I remember someone saying her room is on the first floor, but which way?*

Walking slowly, he bumped into a few things that he hurriedly caught from falling until he found a tall column in the middle of the floor that came out of nowhere. Using it as a guide to move forward, only emptiness followed, nothing tangible to aid the way.

He stepped out on faith, not knowing where he was going. Thumping against a wall, he felt along its hard coldness until he was moving in the direction of a hallway that led him toward the side of the house. A moon light from a bay window landed on a pair of tall, large double doors.

He walked toward the doors and felt for a knob. Slowly twisting it, he pushed the door open just as a lantern was lit and raised.

"Who's there?" Ms. Lora Dean raised the lantern higher. "Tondey. What are you doing in here?"

"I...um..." He dropped his head.

"You come to do me harm, boy?"

"No, ma'am. Um White like you. Why would I—"

"What did you say, boy?"

"I just...I mean. The slaves...ma'am, they've been talking behind your back."

"Who?"

"All of 'em, ma'am."

"What are they saying?"

"That one named Adessa, I heard her tell Black Bean Ray that you're pregnant. The rest of 'em said that the baby's gonna be fat and ugly like you. That's not me saying it, ma'am, that's what they're saying," he lied.

"Hmp...Go on. What else are they saying?"

"They're wondering who the pa of your baby is. They said maybe it's the overseer or some stranger, or..."

"Well...or who?"

"A nig...I mean, a slave. Maybe it's Wink's child, they said."

"What about Paty and Mawbee...they said anything. Lillie, what about her?"

"No, ma'am."

"Anything else. They said anything else?"

"That's about it."

"Get back to bed. I'll deal with this in the morning."

"Yes, ma'am." He turned to walk away but stopped with a dropped head in the direction of the door. "Ma'am, I just wanna say that you can trust me. If they try to do or say anything to do you harm, I'll hurt 'em. I'll hurt 'em all. I'll never let a slave put their nigger hands on you."

"Nigger, huh?"

He looked back over his shoulder. "Yes, ma'am, that's right. Them niggers."

She looked him over. "You're as black as they are."

"Not where it matters most, ma'am."

"Is that right?"

"Yes, ma'am, that's right."

"Hmp...So, you wanna be my savior."

He turned to her. "Yes, ma'am. I'll protect you." Tondey open the door and left.

Easing back into the shack, he got in his bed. With his face to the wall, he smiled. So anxious to see what tomorrow would bring, he didn't sleep.

Chapter 13

As soon as Tondey left the big house, Ms. Lora Dean went to the room Mawbee shared with Lillie and Adessa. She quietly got her out of bed and guided her to the hallway. "Get dressed. We have a run to make. I need you to get the horse and wagon ready."

"Yes, ma'am." Mawbee knew very well where they were going that late in the night. *This can't be for the doctor, 'cause Paty sees about the sick. It gotta be the overseer. What trouble's coming from this?*

That following morning, before the slaves could awaken for work, the overseer stood outside their quarters. "Get out here! Every one of you, out here right now!"

Ms. Lora Dean stood behind him. On one side of her, with lowered heads, were Lillie and Adessa. Paty and Mawbee stood at her other side.

Out front was the overseer, gripping a long, thick whip. Next to him was a tall, slim White man.

The slaves came out of their shacks. Boon and his wife, Laudee. Right after them came Black Bean Ray, Tondey, Wink, and Rudy. They all lined up side-by-side, and seeing the whip, lowered their heads with fear. All except Tondey who stood beside Black Bean Ray, grinning in his heart. His lowered head hid his devious smile.

Stepping from behind the overseer, Ms. Lora Dean paced from one end of the row of slaves to the other. "I hear news been traveling about me. Gossip, bad-mouthing me. It's said that y'all been speaking ill of the one who houses and takes care of you. Better than other masters. Most of you been on this plantation since I've been here. I haven't sold you. Instead, I make sure you have everything you need. I allow you to eat good. Better than some White folks eat. You walk around freer than most slaves... I guess you're too free. Free to run your mouths about business that's not yours."

She stopped pacing and rested her hands on her waist. "This gossip. Talk. It's been here for years. I hear things—always have. And there has always been some new slave trying to get in my good grace by shooting off at the mouth.

"Yeah, my slaves talk, but so what? They do good by me. I never had any problems out of them. They may talk, but I can trust 'em. I can trust 'em with my bedroom door unlocked. I don't worry about any of 'em running off. I don't have to pay an overseer daily to look after any of 'em, 'cause they look after themselves—and me. Yes, they talk. They always talked. They talk about me; they talk about each other. Just like family, they talk. But what they say, stays on this plantation."

She started back pacing in front of them. "Now, I don't like what they always say, but I've never been the kind to care. Until now." Ms. Lora Dean stopped and turned to the tall, slim White man who was standing beside the overseer. "Gone, take care of it."

Every head rose to see whom she'd spoken to and who was going to be *taken care of*.

The slim man walked over to Mawbee, Adessa, Paty, and Lillie.

They immediately dropped their heads. Sweat beads grew on their temples. Each of them recalled what they'd said about Ms. Lora Dean and wondered if they would be the one to be taken care of.

The man continued from them to the other group, leaving the ladies with relieved hearts. He stopped in front of Boon and slowly passed him, halting in front of Laudee.

In fear of his wife being harmed, Boon dropped to his knees and cried out with cupped hands, "Please, sir. It was me. It was me."

Tears rushed down Laudee's face.

"Boon?" Ms. Lora Dean looked at him.

Still wailing, Boon could barely speak. "Yes, ma'am."

"Get up from there!"

"Yes, ma'am," he cried while being helped to his feet by Laudee.

The man continued down the line of slaves. He looked over each of them, slowly creeping, purposefully teasing their fears. Finally, he stopped within inches of one person's face, causing that person internal punishment.

"Well, get it over with," Ms. Lora Dean demanded.

The skinny White man turned to Wink who became so overcome by fear, he tilted into Black Bean Ray who helped him regain his balance. Smirking, the man turned in the opposite direction and went directly for the person he'd been assigned to "take care of." He walked to the group of slaves behind him and grabbed Adessa's arm, pulling her toward his wagon.

"No, no, no, no, no...don't, please, don't. Ms. Lora Dean, I won't say again, I won't say nothing else."

With a hanging head, Black Bean Ray's face tensed. Large veins gathered on his neck. He motioned to move forward, but Rudy, with a lowered head, grabbed his arm. "Don't," Rudy uttered through his teeth.

"Please, ma'am, please. I won't say again! Um sorry!"

"You told my laundry business, gal. There's no forgiveness for that kind've gossip. Gossip has been here since the beginning of time, but some things mustn't be spoken of. You're lucky I don't have the overseer put a whip to you first. But you value more without the lashes. I promised the buyer you wouldn't have slashes on you when delivered, and that's what's saving you. The mighty dollar." Ms. Lora Dean nodded to the man who secured Adessa in the back of a wagon and rode off.

"Black Bean! Black Bean Ray, help me, please!"

"Good riddance!" Ms. Lora Dean turned back to the group of slaves in front of her. "Now, to finish this business of gossip and trust. As I said, you slaves may not love me like family, but I can trust you. You might gossip, but I sleep in peace at night. You take good care of everything on this plantation without me having to tell you to do a thing. Mawbee, laundry duty's been added to your chores until I replace her."

"Yes, ma'am."

"Black Bean Ray?" Ms. Lora Dean called out.

"Yes, ma'am," he rushed to answer.

"Step forward."

Black Bean Ray's heart pounded, not from fear, but anger as he thought about her taking away another woman he loved.

"It was only a matter of time anyway. Every woman I bring on this plantation, you bed 'em. A baby follows right after. You're the reason why I have to keep replacing these laundry girls. This one ran to you with my business. Now, this business regarding me is to be said no more. You mind your tongue."

"Ma'am, I ain't say nothing about it when I learned of it."

"I know." Her voice became soft, solemn. "You've been with me for a long time. You like women, but you don't like gossip. You keep what you know to yourself. That I know. Always did. But you bedded Adessa in front of Tondey. She talked, he heard it and told Wink, who told Boon. That's how it spread." She took a step closer to Black Bean Ray. "The next laundry girl I find, you don't touch. If you do...well, let's just say you'll never have a need to after um done with you. You hear me?"

"Yes, ma'am."

She looked at the overseer and nodded. "Deal with him."

Black Bean Ray dropped to his knees. "Um sorry, ma'am. I won't touch another." Tears rushed down his face.

Ms. Lora Dean stepped aside. "I know."

The overseer snatched him up by the arm.

"Ahh, um sorry, um sorry." As brave as he was, his burst of emotion shook him, making him wail even harder. "Um sorry," he cried.

With his head low, Tondey formed a full-blown smile.

The overseer pushed Black Bean Ray back in the line with the others and grabbed Tondey's arm.

"Wh...wh...what's going on?" Fear in his eyes grew while staring at Ms. Lora Dean. He felt betrayed.

"Tondey, I don't like people I can't trust. If the person you share a shack with can't trust you, how can I? Besides, I told you to never look at me again, and you're standing there right now looking at me." She looked at the overseer. "Teach 'im. Make 'im remember." She walked away.

Mawbee, Lillie, and Paty followed her.

"Paty, it's best you prepare a bed for 'im. He's gonna need it."

"Yes, ma'am."

Chapter 14

"C'mon, C'mon!" Black Bean Ray stood at the door of the sickhouse.

"Um coming." Grabbing his things, Tondey slowly rose from the bed.

"I see ain't nothing changed. You're as slow today as you were before."

"Um just in no hurry to work the hogs."

"Well, they miss you too, Tondey." Black Bean Ray smiled at Paty. "Are you coming for sup tonight? Ms. Lora Dean's gone. She'll be gone for a few days. She said we can stay up as late as we want, as long as we don't slack from our chores."

"I don't know. Sometimes she brings back patients for me to take care of. I have to be ready."

"C'mon now, woman, it's gonna be fun."

"Fun," Tondey said.

Black Bean Ray turned to him. "Yeah, and you got out of the sickhouse just in time to join us." Turning back to Paty, he asked again. "So, are you coming?"

"You know I eat in the sickhouse," Paty said.

"You do...when you have the sick to care for. Um taking your last sick 'til more come. It's time to take care of you. Or let somebody else do it."

She nodded toward Tondey who walked out of the sickhouse on his way to their shack.

"Are you coming?" Tondey yelled.

"Gone. We'll be there shortly," Black Bean Ray said.

"We?" Paty asked.

"Yeah, girl—we." Black Bean Ray walked toward her.

"You know you better mind what you say around him."

"Yeah, I better." He closed the door, grabbed Paty, and pulled her close to him. "You know I love you, right?"

"Black Bean Ray...Adessa's been gone for almost two months. And you and me, we just got started. It's only been a minute. Love doesn't happen that fast."

"Loving you comes easy." He hunched his torso forward against hers. "And started what?" He separated his words with wet neck kisses. "What's that...we done started? Huh?"

"Getting in trouble. Ms. Lora Dean finds out and—"

He stopped kissing her and bent low to gaze into her eyes. "She won't."

"Can't be too careful. So, gone, get out of here before we give big mouth Tondey something to tell her."

Going for the door, he rushed back, and gave her a passionate kiss. "Tonight, Paty. Come sup with us. With me."

She smiled. "We'll see."

He left. "Hey, Tondey, wait up." He caught up with Tondey. "Me and you need to talk."

"Yeah, I know, about Adessa. I—"

Black Bean Ray stepped in front of Tondey, stopping him. "Your mouth got my girl taken away."

"I know, man. Um sorry." He shook his head.

"Sorry ain't gonna bring her back."

"Look, Black Bean Ray. I thought...I was wrong. Um sorry. Um sorry."

Looking in his eyes, Black Bean Ray searched for sincerity. "Yeah, just what I thought, nothing. We'll see how sorry you are when you learn how this plantation works. I think you just learned a little, but something tells me you have a lot more lessons coming." He put his finger to Tondey's chest. "You cross me again, and I'll teach you your biggest lesson." He stepped away from him. "Now, come on, let's go get this sup."

"Hey?"

Black Bean Ray turned around. "What? What's that you have to say?"

"You're forgiving me that easy?"

"Who said I forgave you. I just don't hold nothing against no one. Especially someone in the same position I'm in. But don't take that the wrong way."

"I won't cross you again, man, I won't. You're with Paty now, right?"

"What do you know about it?"

"Nothing. Just treat her right. Do right by her."

"It's not your worry, man. Sup's ready. Worry about that."

Chapter 15

"Man, this a tasty hog." Boon tore into the meat like he was starving.

"You have to know how to raise 'em." Rudy licked his fingers after laying a stripped rib bone on his plate.

"So, it ain't got anything to do with my cooking?" Laudee filled Wink's plate with food and handed it to him.

"It's both of you. There, it's settled." Wink sat at the table with his plate in front of him. "It's perfect and um about to tear into—"

Everyone turned to the door when Tondey and Black Bean Ray entered. Hearing the halt of voices, Tondey eased to the back of the room and sat alone.

Black Bean Ray got a plate of food and sat with the others.

Conversations slowly resumed. A few laughed, some whispered, but most were as loud as they ever were.

Mawbee got up, fixed a huge plate of food, and took it to Tondey. "Here, you need to eat. Aren't you hungry?"

"Yes, ma'am." He took the plate and dug in.

Mawbee sat in front of him. "Tondey, we're slaves. We all belong to the master. None of us are free. In the big house or not, because we don't have no free will to do as we please. As we want to do. That's why slaves have to stick together. This plantation, it's different from others. There's no overseer to watch over us. We don't need one, because we're disciplined. We might fuss, be mad at one another, that's alright. But one thing we never...ever do, and that's turn on each other.

"Ms. Lora Dean, she's White people, but it doesn't matter. She's still people. Human just like the rest of us. She's worse than some, but better than a whole lot, 'til she's not. You brought out the worst in her. Don't do that again, you understand?"

While sucking food from his fingers, Tondey nodded his head but thought about what he had to do to get *the hell off this plantation*.

"No, I need you to really understand me. You ain't seen the worst of her." She sat back and smiled. "And we wouldn't want that to happen."

Ms. Lora Dean walked in. Everyone quickly stood and dropped their heads.

"Well, it looks like I returned just in time."

"Ma'am. Ma'am. Ma'am," they all said.

Mawbee rushed to the shelf and grabbed Ms. Lora Dean's favorite evening dinner plate. It was large, nearly the size of a serving platter. Moving fast, she passed it to Laudee, who began piling food on it.

Boon got her favorite glass, a platter, and its lid.

Mawbee took the platter from Boon.

"Hold on." Ms. Lora Dean turned toward the door and waved forward. "Come on in, dear."

A beautiful mulatto young woman in her late teens came forward.

Tondey's eyes spread wide.

"This here is Mildred. She's our new laundry girl." She looked at Mildred and rubbed her long, curly black hair. "Mildred, this here is your new family. You mind yourself, and they will always be your family. No selling you. No moving from one plantation to the next." She leaned closer to Mildred's face. "And nobody touching you down there." She smiled at the young lady and nodded. "That's Mawbee over there. She'll get you settled in. And Laudee over there," She nodded. "...will fix you a plate of her delicious cooking."

Mawbee walked toward Mildred. "Boon, get Ms. Lora Dean fed." She passed Ms. Lora Dean's platter to him.

"Getting to it this instant."

"Good, because I'm starved. Boon, I'll have it in my room." She left Mildred with the other slaves.

"Yes, ma'am. Bringing it right up." *She always has sup in her room. She's telling me like I'on know.* "Right behind you, ma'am."

Laudee placed the large plate of food on the platter. Boon took it along with a glass of tea to Ms. Lora Dean's room.

Mawbee took Mildred's hand and walked her around the kitchen.

Wink whispered in Rudy's ear. "I still can't tell if she's with child. You?"

"Talking about Ms. Lora Dean? It's like that with big women sometimes."

After introducing Mildred to almost everyone, Mawbee stopped at the end of the table. "Tondey, this here is Mildred."

Tondey was the last one left in the room to be introduced to the new help. He immediately stood, cleaned his hand on his shirt, and reached it out to Mildred. Mildred looked up at the taller, oversized Mawbee as if she needed her permission to take his hand.

Mawbee smiled and nodded.

Turning back to Tondey, Mildred gave him her hand to shake.

Boon returned. "Ms. Lora Dean said to keep the noise down, she's tired. She's gonna eat and rest right after. Mawbee, she'll be needing you shortly."

Mawbee took the plate of food that Laudee brought her and gave it to Mildred. "I have to go tend to Ms. Lora Dean. You gonna be alright?"

"Yes, ma'am." Mildred nodded.

"You can sit with me," Tondey said to Mildred.

Everyone looked at him.

Chapter 16

Some months later, on a nice sunny day, Tondey was called to the porch to see Ms. Lora Dean. Before he could put both feet on the porch, she jumped him with anger. "I wanna hear nothing but the truth from your mouth, you hear me, boy?"

"Yes, ma'am."

"Whose been with Mildred? I know you know something. Spell it!"

Tondey lowered head. "I... Ma'am I don't know who it could be."

"Well, one of you niggers done stuck it where it didn't belong. If it wasn't you, then who was it?"

Tondey was quiet.

"Speak up, boy!"

He jumped.

"Speak up—TELL IT!"

"Ma'am, I..."

"Don't slip out a lie. You do, and I'll pull your tongue out of your mouth and chop it off."

Tondey remained quiet.

"I see...I see. You niggers sticking together...ganging up against me. I'll get you. I'll get every last one of you. MOVE!" Pushing him out of the way, she stormed off toward the door of the house. "I have to get word to the overseer to find me some replacements. Um gonna kill every one of you men niggers and get me a plantation full of women since you men can't keep it in."

Kill us. All of us. "Ma'am!"

She stopped in the doorway and turned to face him. "What, boy? You have something to tell me?"

With shaking dark lips, Tondey rubbed his mouth and let out a deep sigh.

"Spill it, boy!"

"It was mm..."

"Who?" Releasing the door, she walked toward him.

"It was...Black Bean Ray. I saw him sneak with her one night. That's been about—about three months ago. That's about how many months she is."

"How do you know how many months she is?"

"'Cause he said so."

Ms. Lora Dean glared in silence. "Gone get!"

Shaken, Tondey rushed off the porch and sat down to hide behind a huge oak tree. Hours later, the sun was barely visible. Tondey slapped his arm and face and scratched his legs. Swinging his eyes open, he jumped up and discovered that he was the dinner of red ants. He dusted them off and headed for his shack.

The moment he walked in, Black Bean Ray immediately stood. "Hey. I been waiting for you. Where you been?"

Rubbing one foot against the wooden floor, Tondey's face pointed downward to hide his guilt.

"You know what? It don't matter. Here, look what I got you." Black Bean Ray took a plate from his bed. "Laudee fixed this plate of food for you since you ain't come to sup. They're cleaning the kitchen. Said they wanted to get an early start and to bring the plate back tomorrow." Black Bean Ray cast a wide grin. "Look at how much. I told her to pile it on. And look—" Taking a second plate from the bed, he turned to Tondey. "Look what else I got you. Cake. Freshly baked by Laudee." Holding the plates that Tondey did not take, Black Bean Ray frowned. "What's the matter with you?" He put both plates back on the bed.

"Nothing."

"Naw, it ain't nothing, it's something."

Tondey looked at Black Bean Ray. "Since I had Adessa sold, you treated me good. I don't deserve it, Black Bean Ra—"

"Get out of them shacks!" A booming voice came from outside.

"Sounds like the overseer." Black Bean Ray looked out of the small square hole in the wall that they used as a window.

"Get out here! I need all of you out front this instant! Every one of you, get out here right now!"

Coming from their shacks, the scene in their view was all too familiar. Rudy, Wink, Laudee and Boon, all lined up side-by-side with dropped heads. Black Bean Ray and Tondey joined them.

Closer to Ms. Lora Dean were Mawbee, Lillie, and Paty. Mildred stood next to Paty. In front of them was the overseer, standing with his legs apart.

Thoughts pondered. Minds wondered. Which of them would die? They peeped from under their eyelashes and fixed their concerns on the overseer's deadly hip companion. A jagged-edged knife was sheathed on his side. "You!" The overseer pointed. "Get over here."

Everyone lifted their heads and saw that Black Bean Ray was standing in the direction of the overseer's pointing finger. He took a full step forward.

"I said, get over here. You see me over there? I need you here, boy!" He pointed at the ground below him.

No one said a word, but watched in fear. Relieved for themselves, but worried for him.

With growing sweat beads, Black Bean Ray slowly made it to the overseer. "Yes, sir."

Paty looked on in fear. Standing behind Ms. Lora Dean, she leaned toward her and whispered, "Ma'am, what did he do—"

"Quiet!" Ms. Lora Dean turned around and gave Paty a lethal stare.

Looking directly into Ms. Lora Dean's eyes, Paty's widened hers. For the first time, she saw the actual color of Ms. Lora Deans' eyes. *Blue.* Knowing she wasn't allowed to stare, she went to drop her head, but she had stared a second too long.

SMACK!

Paty grabbed her face in shock after Ms. Lora Dean's hand came across it. It was the first time she'd ever felt the physical stain caused by another's hand.

"Don't act uppity with me, gal. No one, I mean no nigger stares me in the face. You hear me?"

"Yes, ma'am." Paty was barely audible. Still holding her face, she dropped her head. Her fallen tears watered the lawn beneath her.

Ms. Lora Dean turned back to the overseer. "Let's get this business done."

"Yes, ma'am." The overseer looked at Black Bean Ray. "Drop 'em, boy."

Black Bean Ray's eyes grew big when looking at the knife that the overseer took from his holster. "What did I do? I don't, I don't under—"

"I said drop 'em, boy!"

"Sir," his voice trembled.

"I won't say it again." The look in his eyes was menacing.

Black Bean Ray took the strings that held his pants on his waist. Unloosing them, his pants slid to his ankles. His dark, muscular butt showed from behind. He quickly cupped his hanging manhood.

With the knife, the overseer signaled, "Move 'em."

Black Bean Ray's hands moved to his side. Closing his eyes, he took a deep breath and braced himself with a balled fist that he forced to relaxed. He placed the palm of his hands on the outside of his legs, but fear grew again. He squeezed in his fists.

The overseer clutched his manhood. Never taking his eyes from Black Bean Ray's eyes, he placed the knife directly on top of his skin next to his pubic hairs. "Since you can't keep it in, um gon' take it off."

With anxious eyes, Black Bean Ray's breathing grew. His chest rose and fell in rapid succession. His fists got so tight, his nails dug into the thickness of his palms. He shook his head from side to side, encompassed with fear. Tears filled his eyes. Steadying himself, he closed his eyes and tensed up while thick tears coursed down his face.

The overseer squeezed tighter. "Look at me, boy."

Black Bean Ray's eyes sprang open.

"You have my permission to look me in the eyes. I want you to see the look of pure satisfaction when I cut it off." With an evil look plastered on his face and the knife planted on the skin of Black Bean Ray's penis, the overseer squeezed harder and grunted.

"Hold up!" Ms. Lora Dean stepped toward Black Bean Ray who was near passing out from nervous anticipation. "My rules are simple. Men keep it in their pants. Women keep their legs shut. But this one, he keeps sticking it where it doesn't belong. Ain't but one way to stop him for good. Overseer, chop it off."

With a crazed grin, the overseer dropped Black Bean Ray's penis, grabbed his testicles, and quickly sliced through the skin with his knife.

The howling sounds of horrific pain rent the air as the overseer held up Black Beans Ray's blood dripping testicles. "He won't get it up again. No more worries about this one, Ms. Lora Dean."

Black Bean Ray collapsed to his knees, holding the bloody area where it leaked down his leg.

Paty motioned forward to help him, but Mawbee grabbed her. "Don't move."

Ms. Lora Dean leaned down to Black Bean Ray's ear. "I won't be selling this gal you've gotten pregnant, but that baby she's carrying is coming out."

In pain and full of emotions, Black Bean Ray cried out.

Hearing what Ms. Lora Dean had said left Paty completely muddled. She frowned in confusion. *I'm not pregnant.*

"Paty!" Ms. Lora Dean called.

"Ma'am."

"I want it out!" She turned and looked at Paty. Her baby blues carried the look of pure evil.

A second wave of confusion washed through her. "Ma'am?"

"Black Bean Ray has gotten her pregnant. Take her in the sickhouse and take it out of her."

Paty looked at Black Bean Ray who'd fallen to the ground on his side, cradling, moaning, and holding the bloody sack where his testicles used to be.

"Wh...who, ma'am?"

The name bled out of Lora Dean's mouth like an unhealed wound dressed in disappointment. "Mildred."

Mildred dropped to the ground. "No, no, no, no, please, don't."

Ms. Lora Dean turned to Mildred who was on her knees begging for mercy with cupped hands. "Didn't I say it, girl—didn't I tell you? What did I say? No relationships, no sex, no babies—didn't I say that when I got you? Didn't I tell you to keep them legs shut?"

"Um, sorry. Um, sorry."

Ms. Lora Dean looked up at Paty and screamed like a mad woman. "TAKE IT OUT!" Turning from them, she raged away but then stopped and swung back around. "And get Black Bean Ray in the sickhouse. Fix 'im up, so he can get back to the field. I want him out in a week's time." Pounding the ground with every step, she headed for the house.

The overseer grabbed Mildred and threw her across his shoulders. He looked at Rudy and Wink. "Get him to the sickhouse."

Chapter 17

In the sickhouse, Paty's hands were full of Black Bean Ray's blood after stitching him up.

He'd passed out from shock and pain.

She sat quietly sobbing.

Mildred sat on the other side of the room listening to Paty weep. "What're you gonna do with me?"

With a dangling head, and a face wet of tears, Paty sniffed and looked up at her. "I have to take the baby out of you."

"But you can't. P-please."

"If I don't, then I'll pay for it. She'll sell me—or kill me. You see what she did to Black Bean Ray, your lover."

"Rudy!" the voice from outside was loud.

Paty quickly stood. "That's her. She's coming!"

Outside of the sickhouse, Rudy raced toward Ms. Lora Dean.

"If I see one more hog running free—"

"Yes, ma'am, you won't. Black Bean Ray and Tondey, they keep 'em in the pen. Now, it's just Tondey. He's having trouble doing it by his-self."

"No excuses, Rudy. I want 'em under control. That one is a mile away from the pen."

"Yes, ma'am. I'll get right to it." Rudy picked up the baby piglet. "This one, he always gets out. Hardheaded."

Inside, Paty had sped into action the moment she had heard Ms. Lora Dean's voice. She rushed to the bed next to Black Bean Ray's bed, where Mildred sat. "Lay in that bed. Hurry up!"

"Huh, wh—"

"Get in the bed like I said. Do it now!"

Mildred stared blankly at her.

Moving fast, Paty snatched the bloody blanket from beneath Black Bean Ray.

He moaned in his sleep from the rough behavior.

She threw a clean blanket over him as she rushed back to Mildred who was still sitting on the bed.

"I said lay in the bed."

Mildred did as she was instructed and Paty threw the blood-drenched blanket on top of her. She dipped a cloth into the bloody bucket of water that she'd used to clean Black Bean Ray and squeezed it out around Mildred and the bed, swiftly drenching the bloody blanket that covered her.

Recalling how a small unborn baby looked from her time with the French doctor, she frantically looked around. "Eggs." She grabbed the plate of left-over eggs from the meal she never got to eat because of the commotion of that morning.

"What are you doing?" Mildred asked.

"Making you a dead baby." She scraped the eggs into the bloody water and slammed the plate back on the table just as the door opened.

Ms. Lora Dean walked in. Her eyes went straight to Paty's bloody hands. "Is it done?"

"Yes, ma'am." Paty lowered her head.

Ms. Lora Dean looked at Black Bean Ray, who had awakened and was moaning again. "Is he gonna make it?"

"Yes, ma'am. He should be ready to get to the field in a month's time."

"I said a week."

"A week. Yes, ma'am. I'll do my best. I—I just can't say if his body will heal that fast."

"You will have him in the hog pens in a week. Healed or not."

"Yes, ma'am."

"We have hogs running around like free slaves—how long for her?" Keeping her eyes on Paty, Ms. Lora Dean never looked at Mildred.

"Ma'am. I—I never took a child out before. I—I can't say."

"I thought you said it was done."

"I think I did—"

"Well, did you or didn't you?"

"I think I did. I can't be sure, but I—"

"You better hope you did." Her eyes moved to the bucket of water that was near Mildred's bed. She walked over and looked down in it. "Is that it?" The bloody eggs had floated to the top.

"It's what I took out, ma'am. With my hands. It's what I pulled out with my hands, but I can't say for sure if—"

"Paty, for your sake, it better be. I don't need you if you can't get done what I've asked of you." Her eyes finally landed on Mildred who kept her face down. "You better hope," she murmured and left the sickhouse.

"When she finds out, she's gonna sell me." Paty sat down on the foot of Mildred's bed. "Or kill me."

Mildred snatched the blood-drenched blanket from her. "Well, you better hope it's done so she won't sell you. Or kill you."

Paty looked at her.

Chapter 18

Mildred had no physical reasons to remain in the sickhouse, but the abortion lie that had been told held her hostage. Night after night, she complained about Black Bean Ray's moans and groans. The pain he had to endure was excruciating. "Why is he still hurting? I thought you fixed him."

"Probably because he was cut with a dirty knife," Paty said.

He burned with fever, was slow to heal, and the rank smell of infection was strong near him.

Paty sat on the side of his bed. Dipping a cloth in a bucket of water, she dabbed it on his hot forehead.

"Mmmh. Mmmh, Mmmh." Black Bean Ray was miserable.

"Can't you get him to shut up? Why is he moaning like that?" Mildred stood looking out the window as if she was in search of someone.

"He's feverish," Paty answered. "And in a whole lot of pain."

"You can't do nothing to stop it?"

"No. He needs a doctor."

Mildred shifted from the window and sat on her bed. "But I heard you were a miracle worker. They said if you can't save 'em, then nobody can."

While still patting Black Bean Ray's head with the cloth, Paty glanced in Mildred's direction. "I'm not a doctor. And I'm not God."

"Well, somebody lied. They talked like you were both."

Black Bean Ray opened his eyes. He spoke with labored breaths. "Paty...I didn't—" He peered at Mildred. "Tell her. Tell her the truth."

Mildred looked at him. "You want me to lie?"

Black Bean Ray tried to sit up.

Putting pressure against his shoulders, Paty tried to push him back to the bed.

"No, I want you to tell her the truth." He looked at Paty. "Paty, I never touched her."

Mildred put a hand on her hip. "What's it to her? You're saying it to her like it matters to her. Wait... Hold on. I get it. You're sleeping with her, ain't you? That's it. Perfect Paty ain't so perfect. Maybe she's pregnant too?"

Paty sighed. "I'm not sleeping with Black Bean Ray."

"Then why were you so sad when the overseer cut off his balls?"

"Because he's my friend. I've known Black Bean Ray for a long time."

Black Bean Ray was still looking at Mildred. "Tell her the truth, Mildred. Tell her I ain't touch you."

Mildred took in a deep breath and sucked her teeth. "No, it ain't his."

"Then whose baby is it?" Paty asked.

Mildred grinned. "If only y'all knew. There's a lot to know, but I ain't telling."

"They cut off my balls for your lie. I wanna know." He moaned.

"Take it easy, Black Bean. You're still healing, and Ms. Lora Dean wants you back in the hog pen in a few days."

He looked at Mildred and said beneath his breath, "I may not know who's the pa, but I know one thing for sure. In a few months, Ms. Lora Dean will know you're still with child. Then there's gonna be a heap a trouble."

"Not just for me." Mildred looked at Paty. "For her too. She was supposed to take it out, remember."

Chapter 19

Evening skies brought on sleepy eyes. Soon after, snoring was heard. The air whispered and bugs buzzed. But it was a nearby sound that awakened Paty. She sat up and reached over to the small table next to her bed. Lighting the lantern, she turned to the bed next to her. "Black Bean Ray?"

"I have to pee."

The thought of privacy came to mind. Paty glanced over at the bed next to his. "Where's Mildred?"

Black Bean Ray looked over at her bed. "I'on know."

"C'mon, let me help you."

"That girl's full of trouble," he said while she helped turn him sideways to pee into a cup. "And she's gonna take somebody right down with her."

"We have to get her to say that it's not your child."

"Yeah."

Paty helped him lay back in the bed and pulled the covers to his waist.

Black Bean Ray grabbed her arm. "Paty, look at me."

"Let me get you tucked in before she comes back." She continued fussing with the blanket.

"Paty, stop. Pat—hey, stop and look at me." He pulled her to sit on his bed. "Paty, baby...um, um less than a man now. I can't ever get it up again. You just held it to help me pee. Used to be when you touch it, it stood straight up...but now, nothing. It ain't gonna do nothing ever again but leak pee. Um no good for you now."

Paty pulled her arm from him and finished covering him up. Taking the cup of pee, she placed it in a corner. "I'll empty it in the morning."

"Paty, you hear me talking to you."

"Yeah, I hear you."

"C'mere."

She walked over and sat on his bed.

"On this plantation, there are no couples. 'Cept for Boon and Laudee, and I think Ms. Lora Dean knows about them. I mean, she allows them to share the same shack, she has to know. She just don't say nothing because they can't have children. But us—those of us who can have children, we can't have a family. We'll die lonely on this plantation. And you, you're too pretty to be lonely. And you're too young. You have too many years ahead of you to be lonely. You need somebody, and I can't be that man for you. Not no more. Are you fine with being lonely on this plantation?"

"I don't know." Her face hung low.

He turned her face to him. "That answer should be no. That's what she do to us and it ain't right. Now, Mildred, she's sneaky, but she's doing what the rest of us wanna do. She's out there somewhere right now with the man who's the daddy of her baby. Probably Tondey, or Wink, or Rudy."

"How do you know?"

"Where else could she be this time of night?"

"Who do you think it is?"

"I can only guess. Out of three men aside from me and Boon, it's one of 'em. And as well as I know each of them, I can't say for sure. And they ain't saying 'cause they don't wanna get in trouble."

"Which one do you think it could be?"

"I'on know, maybe—"

The door opened.

"Where have you been?" Paty stood.

"You mind your man, and I'll mind mine." Mildred went to her bed.

"I told you, me and Black Bean—"

"Yeah, yeah, I heard your lie the first time. No need to repeat it. Ooh, I'm good and sleepy now. Put out that light so we can sleep." She took off all her clothes, giving Black Bean Ray an eye full. "What're you looking at? You can't get it up. Whew, it's hot in here. Or is that me?" She giggled.

Chapter 20

A fall in hog-infested muddy water and Black Bean Ray was back in the sickhouse with an infection. His temperature soared into dangerous territory.

Ms. Lora Dean had always liked Black Bean Ray and regretted her decision to send him to the fields too soon. Concerned, she went to the sickhouse to check on him. "How's he doing, Paty?"

"He might not make it. I can't get his fever down. I've tried everything." Paty wore worry like bad-fitting clothes that were way too big.

"You need any medicines I can get from town?"

"I don't know of any more. But I'm sure there's some out there."

Ms. Lora Dean looked at the anguish Black Bean Ray was in.

"Mmmhh," he mourned.

"Do what you can. I'll get what he needs. We save slaves on this plantation; we don't let 'em die. How would that look on me." She left and returned the following day with a doctor by her side.

Paty stood back with folded arms and worry written all over her face while the doctor treated Black Bean Ray. "I've tried all the medicines I have. I even tried honey and garlic. Nothing's working."

The doctor lifted Black Bean Ray in an upright position and placed a cup to his mouth. "Drink."

Black Bean Ray gulped down the nasty-tasting substance and frowned.

Paty took the cup from him as he lay back down.

"There," the doctor said. "That should do it."

"That's it?" Paty asked. "What did you give him?"

The doctor barely looked Paty's way. Instead, he packed his things and left, leaving no answers or instructions. Definitely not the name of the mysterious liquid he'd given Black Bean Ray.

As soon as Ms. Lora Dean left to catch up with the doctor, Paty rushed to Black Beans Ray's bedside and sat. "How are you feeling?"

Mildred came in. "Um glad he's gone. Black Bean Ray, how are you feeling? You better, now?"

"Mmh," was all he could muster up.

"At least you can make a sound." Mildred gathered her few items.

"What are you doing?" Paty asked.

"Ms. Lora Dean wants me back in the house. Said she have laundry that needs washing. And since um not in the motherly way, I have to get."

"What will you do when she founds out?" Paty questioned.

"I can ask you the same thing."

Paty stood with folded arms. "You have to tell her. Tell her that it's not Black Bean Ray's baby."

"Now, why would I do that? I ain't crazy. That'll get my man in trouble. Get his balls chopped off. Then he'll be no good for me like Black Bean Ray ain't no good for you."

Paty stepped forward in Mildred's face. "And who is your man?"

She looked at Black Bean Ray and smiled. "That's for us to know. I have to go."

The next morning, Paty went to Black Bean Ray's bedside. She felt his forehead and smiled.

He opened his eyes. "Hey."

"Hey." Her smile widened. "You're gonna be all right."

"I think so." He smiled.

"That wasn't a question, Black Bean Ray. That was a fact. You're gonna be all right."

~~~~~

Learning that the healing process wouldn't be rushed, Ms. Lora Dean allowed Black Bean Ray to heal.

A month later, Tondey entered the sickhouse. "C'mon, man. Get out of that bed. Enough laying around being lazy. Time to get you to the hog pen. It's been forever."

"Man, I remember standing right there where you're standing, telling you to get out of this same bed." Black Bean Ray stood and shook Tondey's hand.

"I sure do miss you out there in the pens."

"I bet you do."

"Well," Tondey looked at Paty, then at Black Bean Ray. "I'll see you outside." He backed out of the shack, leaving the two to their goodbyes.

Black Bean Ray grabbed Paty's hand and smiled. "Baby, I just want you to be happy. Ain't no happiness on this plantation. Nothing but work, growing old, and dying with no children."

"What else can I do, Black Bean Ray?"

"You can run. I—I can help you...I don't know, maybe even run with you. But I can't be with you. Not as a man."

"Where is he, Tondey?" They heard Ms. Lora Dean's voice from the outside.

Black Bean Ray dropped Paty's hand and stepped away from her.

"He's getting his things, ma'am." Tondey was loud, hoping they heard the warning of his voice that Ms. Lora Dean was coming in.

"What're you out here for? He doesn't need you to hold his hands. Get back to the pens. He can find his way." She pushed the door open like a force of blowing wind and immediately looked at Black Bean Ray. A relief came across her face. A subtle smile that quickly vanished. "Boy, you're still standing there. Get to the field."

Black Bean Ray dropped his head, sneaked a quick glimpse at Paty, and left.

Ms. Lora Dean waited for the sound of the closing door. She turned to Paty. "Over a month ago, I told you to take it out... Well?"

"Ma'am?"

"Did you?"

"I—I think I did. I don't know. We never had babies on this plantation. Every woman who got pregnant was sold. So, I never had the chance to—"

"Don't get sassy with me, missy. I know my rules. You were with the doctor for what, all your young life and you never saw him take out a baby?"

"No," she lied.

"Mildred's gaining weight. Especially around the gut. Why?"

"I—"

Ms. Lora Dean stepped forward and placed her hand on Paty's stomach. Dropping her baby blue eyes on Paty's stomach, she looked up at Paty. "Are you pregnant too? I hear that you might be."

"Wha...how could I be?"

"I figure you and Mildred have the same baby's daddy."

And who's your baby's daddy?

"That's why I chopped them off, and I'm gonna do the same for every man on this plantation who can still get it up. Except for Boon. I doubt if he still knows what up is." Taking her hand from Paty's stomach, she walked to one of the beds and sat, dipping it with her weight. "I guess I have to get the doctor back here to take it out of both of you." She sighed heavily. "So, it is." She stood and left.

Chapter 21

Black Bean Ray couldn't stand the sounds. The moaning, the groaning, the sounds of lovemaking. And Mildred made sure he heard it all, every satisfying roar, as she sat straddled across Tondey, bouncing up and down against his torso.

Getting up, Black Bean Ray walked out into the night. It was cold, but the wintery air temporarily took away the torturing desire for sex. He looked over at the sickhouse but remembered Paty had received two new patients a couple of days back. "I can't go there."

He turned in the direction of the kitchen and started walking that way but stopped. He ran and hid behind a large oak tree when he saw a man coming from the side of the house where Ms. Lora Dean's office was located. The stranger carried something in his hand, something that he tied to the side of the horse before he climbed on. Black Bean Ray watched the man ride away. Coming from behind the tree, he went to the kitchen and sat.

Moments later, Ms. Lora Dean walked in. "Why are you here?"

Startled, he rushed to stand and lowered his head. "Ma'am."

"You heard me? Say it. What are you doing in here?"

"I...I couldn't sleep."

She walked over to the pantry and started taking out items to make cornbread. "You and me both..." Putting the ingredients on the table, she stopped. "I supposed you saw that gentleman leaving."

"...."

"Get over here and start the oven."

Black Bean Ray did as directed while Ms. Lora Dean began pouring the ingredients into a wooden bowl.

"Well, not that it's any of your business, but he's my doctor. I haven't been feeling too well. No, I'm not pregnant like most of you think. Just got some female issues. But I'll be all right, you never mind me. I'll be all right..." Stirring the ingredients, she stared at nothing. "I just need to get things in order... He said he wanted heirs, my husband. Somebody to leave his fortune to. I have no one. No one to leave...Well, except..." She turned to Black Bean Ray. "Don't worry. I'll do right by you all. I'll do the right thing. Y'all are my children. I just need to figure out how." She looked down and focused on the batter. "You get. I wanna sit here with myself for a spell."

He started walking toward the door while thinking of how cold it was outside. He had nowhere to "get" to, except to the moaning and groaning of sexual activity. He opened the door.

"Hey...no word of what I said. I hear anything and you die."

"No worries, ma'am. I won't say nothing."

"I know you, Black Bean Ray. You always keep things to yourself."

Avoiding her eyes, he looked at her chin and turned to face the outside. "Yes, ma'am. Not one word."

Getting closer to his shack, Black Bean Ray listened for moans, but the night was quiet. He opened the door and walked into Mildred, who was leaving.

"There you are. You left too soon. I was gonna ask to visit your bed, but you left. No matter." She pinched his chin. "You can't get it up anyway."

He slapped her hand away.

She walked away giggling. "What in the world am I gonna tell our child about his daddy who can't get it up? Me and Paty will have that same problem." She left.

He frowned. "What did she say?" Thinking for a minute, he headed for the sickhouse. With a full mind, Black Bean Ray eased the door open to the sickhouse. He tried to avoid disturbing the two injured slaves when passing by their beds. Pulling back the drape that separated Paty's bed from theirs, he stopped on the side of her bed, covered her mouth, and helped raise her from the bed. "Follow me."

She followed him outside where she wrapped her body in her arms. "It's cold." In the light of the night stars, she could see the shine in his eyes that came from building tears. "Black Bean Ray, what's wrong?"

"She's gonna sell you from me," he cried. "She's gonna sell you and our baby."

"Our baby? I'm not pregnant."

He wiped the tears from his face. "But Mildred, she said you—"

"Don't pay her no mind."

"Here I am, half a man, and worried about losing you."

She stepped closer to him. "I'm not going anywhere. I'll probably die on this plantation. An old woman with no children but loving you will be enough for me."

He looked down. Black Bean Ray had always been a man who kept a quiet counsel, never telling a soul what he'd learned or heard. But Ms. Lora Dean's words had disclosed hope.

He looked at Paty. Even though his heart was filled with love, it was still covered in sorrow. *Knowing I can't be the man I want to be to her; I can give her hope.* "Paty, don't let loving me stop you from dreaming of a better life for yourself. Someday, you'll have another life. A husband, children. It won't be me, I know, but as long as I know you're happy, I'll be happy." He wrapped his arms around her waist and suddenly, the coldness was gone and replaced with the warmth that love made.

He looked down, then at her, and smiled. "It moved."

"What moved?"

He looked down again. "It moved."

Chapter 22

A few nights later, Mildred lay in Tondey's bed with her back to him. He pulled her close to him. "You're carrying on like Ms. Lora Dean won't do nothing to you."

"I know stuff about her that nobody else knows."

"Oh, really." He turned her around to face him and wrapped his arm around her back. "What? What do you know about her that we don't?"

"I ain't saying. Especially with Bean listening." She looked over Tondey's shoulder to where Black Bean Ray lay in his bed.

"You hear that snoring? He's sound asleep."

"How do you know? He could be playing sleep."

"Naw, he's asleep. I know that snore. He's dead sleep. So, tell me before I make you."

She wrapped her leg around his hip. "How do you plan to make me?"

"If I start, we're sure gonna wake 'im."

"You know..." She rubbed his hairy chest. "I can barely see you in the dark 'cause you're so dark. With me being so bright, I love me a dark man. I love how dark you are."

"So, you wouldn't love me if I was a White man?"

"Lord knows I wouldn't. I hate White people. Except for..."

"Except for who?"

"My grandma. She's..."

"Yeah...she's what?"

"I have to be getting back."

"Not until you tell me what you were about to tell me."

Mildred got up, got dressed, and walked to the door.

"Mildred. What about your grandma?"

"How can I trust you, Tondey?"

"What do you mean, how?"

"Are you serious? Wasn't it you who told Ms. Lora Dean that Black Bean Ray was the pa of our child?"

Tondey rose in alarm. "Hey, hey. He's right there. An earshot away."

"But asleep, right? Snoring... That means he can't hear when I say that you are the reason he can't get it up. That you were the one who lied, told Ms. Lora Dean that he's the pa of our baby." She opened and closed the door behind her.

He quickly turned to the bed next to him and hoped his eyes were deceiving him. That Black Bean Ray was not sitting up, staring at him.

Chapter 23

The door to the sickhouse opened.

Paty, who was attending to a patient, turned to see who was entering.

"Here are your things. All washed and folded for your patients." Mildred stood holding coverings, cloths, and clothes while looking around. "Where do you want me to put 'em?"

"Put them in the chair," Paty responded.

Mildred placed the folded garments in the chair and walked to where Paty was treating one of her patients. She looked at the man in the other bed. "He's cute. Is she keeping this one?" She looked the man completely over. "Mmmhmm. She needs to keep this one."

Looking at her through face wrappings, the man couldn't speak because his tongue had been cut out, but he could form a minimal smile.

"Uh-uh. I hear you don't have a tongue. I need me a man with a tongue."

His smile dropped.

Mildred looked the other man over. "What about this one?"

"They aren't hers to keep. She's paid to fix them up, then their master will take them."

"That's too bad. I'd love to—" Mildred folded her arms.

"To what?"

"Never you mind... I heard you were raised by a French doctor. That he taught you to take care of patients. He taught you to talk like that too? All proper."

"I suppose I picked it up from hearing him."

"Mmhm. When are you planning to tell Ms. Lora Dean that you're pregnant?"

"Never."

"Never? She's gonna find out in a few months' time anyway."

Paty stopped working on her patient and turned to face Mildred. "No, she will not."

"How do you expect to keep hiding it from her?"

"Mildred, I'm not pregnant. You are, remember."

"Yeah, well, I ain't. So, there."

"What?" Paty stood. "What did you say?"

"I said um not pregnant."

"But...you have to be. Black Bean Ray, he paid the price for you being pregnant."

"Hmp...too bad for him?"

"Why would you say that? And how did Ms. Lora Dean learn that you were pregnant in the first place?

"'Cause I told her."

Squinting, Paty shook her head in disbelief. "You *told* her? You told her that you were pregnant from Black Bean Ray?"

"No—I didn't say by who."

"But you said—"

"No, I didn't say I told her I was pregnant from Black Bean Ray. I said, I told her I was pregnant."

"By Black Bean Ray?"

"No. What, are you dumb or something?"

"So, you're not pregnant?"

"No. And because um not, that means I saved your life?"

"Saved my life?"

"Yes. That means in a few months, my belly won't grow. Remember, she told you to take the baby out. Well, if there's no baby, she'll think you took it out."

"Well, who told her that Black Bean Ray was the father?"

"Ask Black Bean Ray. He knows. He's just not telling you. Bye, Perfect Paty."

Chapter 24

"Get 'im, man, get 'im. You still can't control 'em longest it's been?" Rudy watched in frustration as Tondey chased a rebel hog around.

"He's always getting out. Glad when he's ready for eating. I hope he's worth all this trouble." Tondey picked up the piglet and walked it back inside the pen. "There's always one rebel in the bunch of babies."

"C'mon, let's call it a night. Make sure you lock the gate tight this time."

"I will." Tondey secured the gate.

Ignoring Rudy, Black Bean Ray walked off in silence, the opposite of his usual friendly personality.

"Hey, Black Bean Ray, wait up." Wink jogged to catch him as Black Bean Ray slowed down.

"Why's your mind so far gone?"

"I'on know."

"Sure, you know. You've been this way all day."

Black Bean Ray looked down at the shorter Wink, who was like a brother to him. They'd come to the plantation only a week apart when Ms. Lora Dean's husband was taking care of sick slaves. Considered troublemakers on their last plantation after both had lost close relatives to death and being sold, the young, teenage boys bonded like brothers.

Ms. Lora Dean didn't want any relationships on her plantation, so she moved Wink out of the cabin he shared with Black Bean Ray to live with Rudy after the helper who lived with him had died.

Looking at his friend, Wink knew something was wrong. He glanced behind them, saw Rudy and Tondey walking side by side, not close enough to hear their conversation. "What's wrong with you?"

Black Bean Ray stared ahead while walking. "It's Paty...she's pregnant."

"And it's yours?"

Black Bean Ray looked down at him. "Of course, it's mine. Who else's is it gonna be?"

"I'on know. Tondey was in the sickhouse a few times. Then there are new men she gets to take care of all the time. I mean, I know you like her, but, you know, Black Bean, you like a lot of women. Mostly the laundry girls, but never her in that way."

"Not at the same time, Wink. I never liked them at the same time, you know that."

"Then there's the other thing."

"What other thing?"

"You know. You've been cut down there. I didn't know you could still—"

"She got pregnant before that happened. And I can. It moved. I haven't tried it yet, but I think I can. I think the overseer didn't cut it right."

"Why did you get involved with Paty? You know that's gonna be trouble for you."

"It just happened. When I hurt my finger that time and had to go to the sickhouse. It just happened. I didn't try to like her that way 'cause I didn't wanna lose nobody else to Ms. Lora Dean selling them off. But with her it just happened."

"Well, it's trouble now, 'cause you say she's pregnant."

"Yeah, but she says she's not."

"How do you know she is if she says she not?"

"I don't know."

"Paty ain't known for lying."

"I think she's trying to protect me. So, she won't tell me. If she is, um gonna make her run. I can't let Ms. Lora Dean sell her from me."

~~~~~

The moment Rudy entered the kitchen, Boon jumped him with questions. "Who's pregnant, Rudy? One of 'em, both of 'em, all of 'em?"

"I figure y'all know more than me." Rudy headed for a plate.

"Naw. Mawbee, you know she's tight-lipped. Said she'll tell us when she knows, but then don't say nothing about it since that day."

Mawbee entered the kitchen just as Tondey, Black Bean Ray, and Wink walked in.

"Laudee, Ms. Lora Dean will take her supper now. She wants extra this time."

"Extra?" Boon went for the larger plate and platter and handed it to Laudee.

"She's had extra before, Boon, ain't nothing new about it." Mawbee filled the sterling silver teapot with tea and grabbed a glass. "I'll be back to get the platter of food."

As soon as she left, Boon turned to the men. "Laudee fixes her a whole heap. Always has because she's a big eater, y'all know that. Why's she asking for extra when she don't know what extra is? Extra be on her plate always."

"She's pregnant." Tondey grabbed a plate and waited for Laudee to fill it.

"What you know about it, Tondey? Who said?" Boon asked.

"Um just guessing like the rest of you."

After Laudee had filled the other plates, Black Bean Ray handed her two plates. "Here, Laudee. Fix Paty a plate, so I can take it to her."

Mildred entered the kitchen.

"Boon already took three plates to the sickhouse. One for Paty," Laudee responded.

Mildred grabbed an empty plate from the table. "Yeah, she don't come out much since she's been caring for them two men over there. I think one of them has taken a liking to her. Maybe she's liking him back."

Still holding two plates, Black Bean Ray tensed up.

Laudee took one plate from him. "Told you, you don't need but one."

Seeing that he was bothered, Mildred stood next to him, waiting for her food. "She's right, you only need one. Paty don't need food.

She don't need nothing. With them men in the sickhouse, she has all she needs. She don't need anything from you." She dropped her eyes to Black Bean Ray's private parts. "Nothing."

Black Bean Ray tightened his lips and turned toward the door.

Wink stepped in front of him. "Hey, hey, don't. Let her talk. She's just trying to get to you."

Black Bean Ray looked over Wink's head. "Hey, Tondey, get your woman."

"I knew it. I told you, Laudee. That's Tondey's baby," The satisfying news lit up Boon's eyes.

"Baby? Um not pregnant."

Tondey stood. "But you said you were. You told me you were. You're gaining weight around the belly. Why?"

"The weight comes from Laudee's good cooking. I told you there're things going on that none of you know nothing about." She turned to Laudee. "Um waiting for my food." After Laudee filled her plate, Mildred left the kitchen.

Tondey flopped in the chair.

"This is a mess, Laudee." Boon stuffed food in his mouth. "Well, at least we know she's not pregnant."

After fixing her plate of food, Laudee joined them at the table, sitting next to Boon. "Do we? That child is messy. And she lies. Always lying."

"So, maybe she is pregnant. Is that what you're saying, Laudee?" Wink felt the need to ask for Tondey who was sitting quietly. Obviously, disappointed.

"Maybe. Soon we'll know. If she is, she can't hide it forever." Laudee put food in her mouth."

Chapter 25

"You leave me alone, old man. Get out of here. Leave me alone."

It had been a while since the old figure stood watching Tondey. "What you want? Every time you come, something bad happens. What bad news are you bringing this time?"

The old man said nothing. Never had. Always just holding Tondey in his sight, causing him to wonder what horrible fate was coming.

"If you won't say, then get. I said get—get out of here!"

Black Bean Ray awakened and sat up. "Who're you telling to get?"

"Nobody." Tondey had grown afraid to gaze directly into the glaring shines of the old man's eyes. So, he glanced in the corner to see if he was still there.

"You're telling somebody to get out? Since um the only one here, it must be me."

"Nothing. Nobody. Talking in my sleep, I guess."

Black Bean Ray stood, slipped on his pants, and tied the strings.

"What're you doing? You're going somewhere?"

"Yeah. I have to pee. That's the only thing that comes out of my hole since you told Ms. Lora Dean that it was me who got Mildred pregnant."

"I ah...man. About that...I was scared. I didn't know she was gonna have that done to you."

"What did you think she was gonna do? Shake my hand? Congratulate me?"

"I'on know. I didn't think. I was scared."

"It's that last part that explains everything. Nothing else mattered. Nobody mattered. I didn't matter. 'Cause you were scared, I didn't matter. I ough'ta break your face." With a balled fist, Black Bean Ray stepped closer to Tondey.

"You're right. I was wrong. I...you've treated me nothing but good, and I lied on you to save me. To save my ass. Do want you want to me, you have the right. I deserve it." Tondey dropped his head and shook it.

"I thought about it. But killing you...Ms. Lora would've killed me. Not 'cause she loved you, but 'cause that makes her lose money. And you ain't worth my death. I'll let God deal with you. I gotta pee."

Mildred was on her way to visit Tondey when she saw Black Bean Ray leaving. "Where's he going?'"

Black Bean Ray took the path to the sickhouse.

"No sense of visiting Paty. You ain't got nothing to please her." Making her way to their shack, she eased the door open and closed it behind her.

Tondey had turned onto his side, facing the wall.

She slipped into his bed and pressed herself against his back.

"Hey, man, what..." He looked behind him. "Oh, it's you."

"Yes, it's me. And there's you, and now, it's us." She pulled him onto his back, she climbed on top so she could look down at him. The tiny window provided some light.

"Black Bean Ray's coming back shortly," Tondey said.

"No, he's not. He's gone to the sickhouse to see after precious Paty. See if that baby of hers is his."

"Why'd you do that, Mildred?"

"Do what?"

"Tell him that Paty has everything she needs since she has men patients to tend to."

"'Cause it's true. Precious Paty ain't no saint."

"What about you?"

"What about me?"

"Are you pregnant or not?"

Leaning forward, she swung her leg behind her and fell on her back.

He turned on his side to face her. "Well, are you?"

"I told you, there's so much you don't know."

"So, are you gonna tell me or not? You keep talking about what we don't know, then enlighten us. Tell it."

"En-en-lite."

"Enlighten. It means to tell something you know that we don't."

"Where did you learn that from?"

He smirked. "Another life. Well..."

"Well, what?"

"Tell me what it is that I don't know."

"I can't. But I can..." She climbed back on top of him.

He touched her stomach. "At least tell me if you're pregnant."

"I don't know."

"What do you mean, you don't know? A woman knows if she's pregnant."

"Paty did something to me. She's not sure if she got it out or not."

Tondey sat up. His hands went to her shoulders. "So, you were. You were pregnant and Ms. Lora Dean, she made Paty kill our child?"

"I don't know if I was before then."

Looking at her, he didn't know what to believe.

"I wish I was, 'cause you're so dark." Placing her hand on his hairy chest, she rubbed. "I want a baby as dark as you to get rid of all this light skin for good."

Tondey moved her off him and sat on the side of the bed.

"What's wrong?"

He looked in her direction. "If you are pregnant, our child and you being mixed with Black blood...me being so dark. Our baby will be black."

"Not all black. I have half-White blood in me. Too bad all the White blood won't be gone, though."

He turned from her and looked in the corner where the old man stood quietly observing. Why are you here? Something is about to happen, isn't it?

Chapter 26

The baby came out crying the moment it entered the world.

Paty smiled while holding the big, healthy boy in her arms. It was what she'd always secretly wanted. A thought she'd never shared with anyone. Smiling at it once more, she placed the baby boy in its mother's arms and went to the door to call for Tondey. He'd gotten word that the baby was coming and had stood outside waiting. "Come on." She waved him in.

Tondey slowly walked into the sickhouse and eased up to the bed where Mildred held their baby boy.

She looked at him, then the baby. "Here he is. Your lil' boy."

Tears welled in his eyes. He and his wife in his past life had always wanted a baby and had tried for years with no success. He figured it was him who couldn't have a baby because he'd been with other women and had never gotten any of them pregnant. But now, "There he is." Tondey took the baby boy from Mildred's arms and cradled him. Staring into those tiny bright eyes, tears fell down his face. *I can have children.* He huffed out a giggle.

Paty walked over. "Let me take 'em. I have to get him fixed up. Ms. Lora Dean will be over soon. This is the first baby on the plantation. I want her to be happy about it. About him." Just as she was about to take the child from Tondey, Ms. Lora Dean and the overseer walked in.

"So, it's your baby. It's your child and not Black Bean Ray's." Her eyes were securely on Tondey, who quickly dropped his head while Paty took the baby.

"You had me cut off Black Beans Ray's manhood for your lie, boy? You made him pay for your cowardness."

Paty took the baby to the other side of the room.

Tondey stood alone with a lowered head.

"Speak, boy!" The sharpness in her voice caused him to twitch and the baby to cry.

"Ma'am, I..."

"No, need for another lie. Black Bean Ray probably deserved it. He had me sell off all my laundry girls 'cause he couldn't keep it in. But he's no liar. Sure enough ain't no coward." She nodded to the overseer.

He and his helper rushed and grabbed Tondey and took him outside.

"What y'all gonna do to him?" Mildred's eyes grew fearful.

"You mind your own business. I'll deal with you later." She looked at Paty who was cradling the child. "And that baby."

Mildred got out of the bed and stood in front of Paty and the baby, blocking them from Ms. Lora Dean's view. Blood from her womb rushed down her legs. "If you do, I'll tell. I'll tell everybody."

Ms. Lora Dean stepped forward and stopped in Mildred's face. "Don't test me, gal. Don't you ever test me!" She grabbed Mildred's neck and squeezed. "I should snuff the life out of you right now.

Bringing this trouble to my plantation. I should have sold you instead of bringing you here to bring me trouble. You be glad I didn't sell you, gal." She released Mildred, who coughed and gasped for breaths.

Stepping around her, Ms. Lora Dean looked at the baby.

Paty looked up, being careful not to be noticed. *Is that a—? It is... She's smiling. She just doesn't want anyone to know, but she's smiling.*

Ms. Lora Dean turned and stormed out of the shack.

About ten minutes later, wailing woke up those who were asleep after battling the heat and bugs that refused to let them rest. The howling and screams unsettled their ears and forced them from the uncomfortable beds that were filled with straw and cotton and covered with blankets.

They opened their doors and witnessed a whip coming across the back of Tondey. One lash at a time, that seemed to never stop. They watched as his flesh was ripped apart, split, and bled until his head slumped over.

"That's it. He's dead," Wink said, standing next to Rudy.

"Naw, shock got 'im."

Even in his unconscious state, the whip continued until, "That's enough." Ms. Lora Dean nodded.

The overseer took his knife from its holster, walked to Tondey's dangling unconscious body, and cut the strings of his pants. They dropped to his ankles. Taking Tondey's manhood in his hand, and with a quick snip, the vessel that had made Tondey the father of a newly born boy was amputated, stopping him from ever making another child. The overseer held it high. "What do you want me to do with it?"

"Put it in his fibbing mouth."

In the sickhouse, Paty and Mildred quickly turned toward the door when it opened.

Ms. Lora Dean walked in, stood in the doorway, holding it open. "Paty, get Mildred ready. I want her out of here by tomorrow. I'm gonna need that bed. I have a man on his way. He tried to run, stepped on a trap that ripped up his foot. He'll be here tomorrow. Get that bed ready for him. Mildred, I need you back to work. Laundry don't wait on resting hands."

Mildred sat on the side of the bed cradling her small, wrapped infant. She watched as Black Bean Ray and Wink walked into the sickhouse with Tondey's arms stretched across their shoulders. They were clenching his dangling hands to keep him lifted until laying him on a bed.

"What's that in his mouth?" Realizing what it was, Mildred leaned over and gagged, nearly vomiting, almost dropping her newborn baby.

Paty rushed to take the child from her. The second the baby was out of Mildred's arms, she ran toward Ms. Lora Dean and pounded her chest. "What did you do to him? What did you do?"

The overseer and slaves looked on in shock.

Ms. Lora Dean grabbed Mildred's wrist and pushed her back on the bed. With a drawn hand, she slapped and knocked her to the floor.

Mildred dropped her head and cried.

The overseer put his whip out front, ready for the order he knew would be given by Ms. Lora Dean to take the whip to Mildred's back.

Ms. Lora Dean rushed off, leaving everyone but Mildred stunned.

That night, while Paty, Mildred, and the baby slept in the sickhouse, Tondey lay nude, propped on his side to keep the cuts on his back from sticking to the bed. He mourned in agony and subconsciously grabbed the area where the pain heavily resonated. His eyes swung open when he realized, "It's gone."

Studying him from the corner of the room was the old man.

Tondey looked pass him and saw that Paty, Mildred, and the baby were sound asleep. He tried to raise up but was stopped by a rolling wave of agony. He looked at the old man again. "You, coot. You old coot. You old...What did you do to me? Why do you keep doing this to me?"

Tondey's frustration with the old man woke up Mildred and the baby. Then, Paty. "You old, coot. Why are you doing this to me? Why?"

They stared at him.

"He's delirious. Trauma got him," Paty said.

Chapter 27

Months went by with sick and injured slaves coming and going and keeping Paty busy. After the last slave she'd treated was healed and sold, she breathed a sigh of relief. "Finally, I have the time I need to reorganize the sickhouse." She stopped to rest in her favorite chair, one that had been built by Black Bean Ray years back.

Ms. Lora Dean walked in. "Paty, I have a girl coming. A runner who's been beaten nearly to death after being caught. I haven't decided if I want to keep or sell her since she's all bruised up. You know it's hard to get a decent dollar for them like that." She dropped her head in thought. "Guess I need to see how she heals." She looked up at Paty. "Do what you can to fix her up, and I'll decide after."

"Yes, ma'am."

That night when the new girl arrived, Wink was tasked to help Paty get her in the bed.

"Wink, you can lay her in that bed," Paty instructed.

Wink cupped the woman in his arms while she slept. He was completely enamored by her beauty. "That peach skin," he whispered.

"Wink. Wink! Put her in that bed."

"Huh. Oh, yeah." Even after laying her down, her beauty kept him mesmerized. He couldn't take his eyes off her.

"Pass me that splint hanging over there."

"Where?"

"Right behind you. Hanging on the wall."

He looked around.

"That stick near the corner over there."

Taking the stick from the nail, he gave it to Paty.

"Thank you. You can leave now. I need to get her changed."

He stood there, looking down at the woman.

"Wink. Wink! You can leave now. I have to change her."

"Oh, yeah. Okay. Um gone." He stood a moment longer, staring at the beautiful woman.

"Wink!"

"Okay, um leaving." Walking away, Wink kept his eyes on her, bumping into the wall near the door. Still watching her, he felt his way out the room.

~~~~~

A month later...

"Ain't it enough? You didn't learn from them, Wink?"

"I can't help my heart, Rudy. She's pretty. And smart."

"And trouble, don't forget that. She ain't gonna be nothing but trouble for you. I can tell you that now." Rudy hung up his tools, and he and Wink headed for the well to rinse off the mud and dirt. Fully dressed in their work clothes, one pumped and the other rinsed. They switched and then afterward, went back to their shacks to change into the only set of changing clothes they had and headed for the kitchen.

The conversation being held in the kitchen met them the moment they walked in. Boon was in his normal full force of gossip. "I'on understand it. What's so special about *that* girl? She's high-yellow, but so was all the other laundry girls."

"And she's sassy, too. She got a real sassy mouth... And lies. I ain't never heard nobody lie so much in all my days." Laudee lifted the lid from the hearty soup pot and stirred.

"Is the food ready yet, Laudee?" Rudy walked near the stove. "Sure do smell good."

"Be so shortly," Laudee answered.

"Ms. Lora Dean named the baby yet?" Rudy grabbed a bowl that was piled on the table and stood waiting for his helpings.

"Not that I can say," Boon responded.

Mawbee entered the kitchen. "Ms. Lora Dean's ready for her servings, Laudee."

"Be a few," Laudee answered.

Boon walked toward the dishes. "Let me get her bowl. She wants the regular big helpings or the one bigger than that one?"

"You ain't funny, Boon. The regular one will do just fine."

He grabbed the larger bowls from the shelf. "They're all two-men size bowls if you ask me."

"I ain't ask you, Boon. Just get the bowl and hand it to Laudee."

He did as he was told.

"Mawbee, did Ms. Lora Dean name that baby yet? It's almost six months. She ain't never waited that long to give a name." Rudy was still waiting with his bowl. "I hear she called the boy, Baby. That's what she's gonna name him, Baby?"

"She decided on Walt." Mawbee responded. Tondey and Black Bean Ray entered the kitchen.

"On what? What's that she's calling 'im?" Boon questioned again.

"Walt!"

"Yeah, who's calling?" Tondey looked around after hearing the name he'd commonly answered to.

All eyes went to him.

"Your name ain't Walt, Tondey," Wink said. "Ain't nobody talking to you. That's the baby's name. Mawbee just said so."

"It's name's Walt?" Tondey questioned.

"Yep. That's the name Ms. Lora Dean gave 'im," Wink answered. "A Black baby named Walt. Ain't that something?"

"It ain't just Black, Wink, it's got White in it too," Tondey argued.

"You're gonna find out that it don't matter how much White he has in him. He's still a slave," Boon said.

Holding his bowl, Rudy was still waiting for his servings. "Ain't that the truth. Best thing having White in 'im might get him is housework. But it's all slave work just the same."

"The food's ready." Laudee took the lid off the huge pot and filled Ms. Lora Dean's bowl.

Black Bean Ray got his bowl after Mawbee left with Ms. Lora Dean's food and stood in line behind Rudy.

After Rudy's and Black Bean Ray's food were fixed, they sat. The next in line walked up carrying two bowls.

"Why do you have two bowls, Wink?" Laudee took one of the bowls and filled it.

Yelling from the kitchen table, Rudy answered with a mouth full of food. "For that girl in the sickhouse. He ain't learned nothing. Tell 'im Tondey. Black Bean Ray, talk to your friend. Ain't no woman worth that being cut-off. Tell 'im."

"They ain't worth it." Tondey picked up a bowl and stood behind Wink.

Wink looked over his shoulder at Tondey. "Then why are you still running after Mildred when Ms. Lora Dean's keeping her from you?"

"I ain't trying to see her. I just wanna see my son. I ain't seen him since Mildred left the sickhouse. The baby's about a half-year old and I ain't seen 'im since he was born."

"And you might not ever see 'im." Boon grabbed a bowl and got in line behind Tondey.

"What do you mean?" Tondey turned behind him to Boon.

"Word has it that Ms. Lora Dean is gonna sell 'im."

Chapter 28

"You think so?" Wink hung the tools just before knock-off time.

Black Bean Ray waited. Normally one to keep his thoughts to himself, he didn't want what had happened to him and Tondey to happen to Wink. "I know so. Why do you think she bring all these pretty light skin women here? She's just mean. She knows we're gonna take a liking to 'em. We get 'em pregnant, she sells 'em off, *with* our babies in their bellies and do it all over again with the next girl she brings. She goes out and finds the most beautiful girls. They're never ugly. Always small and mixed with White. She can find light skin Black girls, but she gets them mixed with White. Why? It don't matter their color. We'll like 'em no matter their skin color."

"I think she changed after Mildred. She didn't sell her," Wind mentioned.

"Yeah, and I wonder why that is."

"And she won't let Tondey see the baby. It's half a year old and she ain't let that man see his child. Why? It's his."

"She's mean, I tell you. Just mean." Black Bean Ray headed for the well to rinse up.

Wink followed.

Later, they met everyone in the kitchen.

While getting her plate of food, the new girl, Yellow, who had limped from the sickhouse to the kitchen, batted her eyes at Wink and sat at the end of the long table where no one had congregated.

Wink smiled at her, grabbed a plate, and got in line.

Black Bean Ray bumped Wink's arm and leaned closer to his ear. "Don't forget what we talked about earlier."

"Oh, yeah." Taking his eyes from Yellow, he straightened himself and looked forward.

The moment Mildred entered the room, Tondey stood up from his plate of food. She walked over to him. "How's he doing?" he rushed to asked her.

"Our lil' green eyes boy is perfect."

"Green eyes. His eyes are green?"

"Yeah. Green pretty eyes. They didn't start green. I thought they were gonna be gray, but then they turned green. I'on know if they'll stay that color."

"They will."

"How do you know?"

"I just know."

"When are you coming to see 'im?"

"As soon as the light goes out in Ms. Lora Dean's room. She leaves it on all night. I think on purpose."

Mawbee walked into the kitchen.

Mildred quickly left Tondey to grab a plate and get in line.

Mawbee skipped them all as usual.

Boon was already handing Ms. Lora Dean's plate to Laudee to fill. "I have her pot of tea and cup right here, Mawbee." Boon gave it to Mawbee. He covered the plate on the platter and followed her out of the kitchen.

Tondey watched Mildred get her food and leave. She never bothered to look at him again as if she'd been warned.

After getting his plate filled, Wink turned in the direction of Yellow.

"Wink, I know you ain't going over there? She knows she supposed to eat at the sickhouse." Black Bean Ray shook his head.

"Um just seeing what's going on with her." He walked her way.

"Wink...Wink!"

Ignoring Black Bean Ray, Wink stopped in front of Yellow. "You know the color yellow is my favorite color?"

"And I didn't like that name she gave me until now. When you said it."

"I didn't like that color until you got it for your name."

"C'mon, sit with me."

Wink sat. "How long you staying? Ms. Lora Dean say?"

"I'on know. My massa, he said if I return, he's gonna send me to the field to work."

"Well, she's named you now. She won't do that unless you're hers. You're high-yellow, that means you'll be in the big house. You've been in the big house before?"

"Yeah."

"The big-house work is easy. Nothing like the fields. I heard you ran. Why?"

She lowered her head. "'Cause my massa...he kept coming after me. I see how he treats children born to him. He puts them in the field and works 'em real hard. Like he's punishing them for being his. He has them beaten, too." Staring blankly at nothing, she shook her head. "I don't want that for my child. Beaten and worked because it's his. Two of his children he had beaten to death. It's not right." She looked down at her stomach and rubbed it.

Wink leaned in and whispered. "You're pregnant?"

"About a quarter way 'til birth." Rubbing her stomach, she smiled.

"There're no babies born on this plantation. Except one and we don't know how long it'll be before it's sold. It's been half a year, but we think it'll be gone soon."

"Where my baby goes, I go. Even death."

Sitting back, Wink rubbed his mouth. *Rudy's right. She might be smart, knowing how to read and all, and she sure is pretty, but like Black Bean Ray said, she's nothing but trouble for me.* Picking up his fork, he swooped food from his plate into his mouth with speed.

"You starving or something?"

"No, I have more chores to do."

"But it's dark out. What chores do you have to do in the dark?"

"Sometimes the pigs get out. I need to make sure everything is locked down."

"Don't you do that before you leave the pen?"

"Yeah, but somehow they find ways to get out." Standing, he took his plate to Boon for cleaning and left in a hurry.

Chapter 29

"Who's that?" Because of the baby, Mildred had been given a private room. She lived in one of the four bedrooms in the large, two-story house. She rose from her bed as the door crept open.

"Shhh. Be quiet."

She sat up and lit the lantern. "Tondey...Ms. Lora Dean's gon—"

"Shhh." Tondey rushed to the wooden cradle that Black Bean Ray had made after Mildred had given birth.

"What you doing here?"

He reached in to get the baby.

Mildred walked over to him. "What you doing? Put him back." She grabbed his arm.

Releasing the baby, he turned to her and sighed. "Mildred, we're running. Now, if anybody can survive out there, it's me. I know a lot about the woods. I know things that can help us get far away from here. Things I learned growing up and living in the country years back."

"I ain't running, Tondey."

"Why? If you don't, she's gonna sell the baby. Are you alright with that?"

"She ain't gonna sell my baby."

"Why are you so sure?"

"'Cause it's...she ain't gonna sell 'im, and I ain't running. I ain't going out there in the woods with no baby in tow. All them bugs, snakes, and swamps. Bears. There're bears out there. I ain't the running type."

"I have this lil' human being that I can't even see. My blood's running in his veins. I ain't never been so in love with nothing or nobody 'til I saw his lil' face. We live on the same plantation, and I can't see 'im. My first and only child, who's only steps away from me, and I can't see 'im. Now, I hear she's gonna sell 'im."

"She's not gonna sell 'im."

"How'd you know? How can you be so sure?"

"Trust me, I know."

"No, tell me. If not, um taking him and running. You can stay, but um taking my son and running."

"I don't have to tell you nothing, and you ain't taking my baby."

"What right do you have, huh? You're a slave like me. You get to see 'im, but I can't. Why, Mildred? What's so special about you that's different from the rest of us?"

There were only a few times Tondey had stared Ms. Lora Dean in the face and looking at Mildred, the memory of her distinctive features came hastily. He couldn't take his eyes off Mildred's chin, her nose.

"What're you looking at?"

"There it is. That's why. It's been there all this time and I ain't seen it 'til now."

"Seen what?"

"Yeah, I never paid attention 'cause White folks don't allow no Blacks to stare at them. I see why. It's because their faces show all their secrets. That's where their secrets are, in their faces."

"Secrets. You're talking crazy."

"No, um making sense. It's all making sense now. That same dimple Ms. Lora Dean got on her chin, you got on yours."

"Dimple?"

"Yeah, that dent right there." He touched her chin.

She knocked his hand away, walked to the bed and sat.

"I stared at Ms. Lora Dean's face before. I remember that hump on her nose. It's just like the one you have on yours. Yours is much smaller, but it's there. Mildred?"

"What?"

"You're Ms. Lora Dean's child, ain't you? But how? Because you have Black blood in you. Unless."

Chapter 30

A knock so soft made Black Bean Ray and Tondey question whether someone was at the door. They both sat up in their beds, looked at each other and then the door.

"Open up." The whispering voice that came from outside was faint but confirmed the visitor.

Black Bean Ray opened the door and was nearly pushed out of the way by Boon, who was nearly out of breath.

Tondey jumped out of bed. "What's wrong with you? Why're you out of breath?"

Boon bent over, gasping with his hands on his knees. "Hold on. Have to...I have to catch my breath." He huffed a few times and stood, still out of breath. "Your baby..."

"Yeah, my baby, what about my baby?"

"Ms. Lora Dean..."

Tondey made a circular hand motion to rush Boon to speak. "C'mon, old man, spit it out."

"She sold your baby."

"What?" With eyes fixed on Boon, Tondey pushed him out the way and went for the door but was stopped by Black Bean Ray. "What're you planning?"

"Um gonna—"

Boon interrupted Tondey. "There's nothing to do. The baby's been gone for two days. We're just now learning of it."

"Two days and we're just finding out!" Black Bean Ray stepped away from the door and turned to face Boon.

"Well, see...Ms. Lora Dean, she had Paty give Mildred something to help her sleep."

"Paty!" Tondey's eyes widened.

"Hold on, now. Paty, she was just following orders. Ms. Lora Dean sent Mawbee to fetch the stuff from Paty. That's all Paty knew. That she was sending Mildred something to help her sleep."

"So, Mawbee knew?"

"Well, see, Tondey. You have to understand that Mawbee, she knew what she was fetching. Something to help Mildred sleep, 'cause Mildred said she ain't rest much 'cause the baby be up crying all night. Mawbee gave the stuff to her and took the baby with her back to her room so Mildred could rest. The other night, while Mildred was asleep, and the baby was with Mawbee, Ms. Lora Dean went in Mawbee's room and got the baby. Mawbee didn't know what was going on 'cause Ms. Lora Dean took the baby from the cradle and didn't say why. The next day, Mawbee thought that the baby was with his ma until Mildred woke up asking about her baby. Mawbee told her that Ms. Lora Dean took the baby. Mildred got mad and went after Ms. Lora Dean, hitting her. Then Ms. Lora Dean sent for the overseer to come after Mildred."

"Come after Mildred!" Tondey was fuming. "I saw Mawbee in the kitchen yesterday and today. She didn't say nothing to me about it. None of y'all did."

"Hold on, now. See, we didn't know anything until Mawbee came in the kitchen tonight to fetch Ms. Lora Dean's food. We thought it was strange because it was so late. She came after everybody had eaten when we were cleaning. It made us mad because we had to get the food hot again. Mawbee turned to leave, and I stopped and asked her why so late. She didn't tell me anything, but I could tell that something was on her mind, something heavy, but she wouldn't say."

"Me and Laudee, we had to wait for Ms. Lora Dean's dirty dishes to clean them before we could leave the kitchen. Finally, Mawbee came back down bringing Ms. Lora Dean's dirty dishes. She handed the dishes to Laudee. Her hands were shaking something terrible, and that's when she told us."

"So, fear made her tell. Because she was scared, she told."

"Tondey, what's she gonna say? She's in the big house, but just like us, Ms. Lora Dean's her massa. She answers to her, not us. Least of all, not you. Fear made her scared like it does all of us."

"You should understand that better than anybody. Look at what your fear got me." Black Bean Ray looked down at his pants.

Tondey thought for a moment. "I can't worry about that right now." Going toward the door, he gave it a harder shove and stormed out.

Black Bean Ray ran behind him. "Hey, hold up." He grabbed him, but Tondey fought to get loose.

"Why are you grabbing me? Look at us. Me dick-less, you ball-less, neither of us have women, and she's taken away the one thing that means something to me." Tondey's eyes shined with fury. "I'm gonna kill her, Black Bean, and ain't nobody gonna stop me. Not even God. And definitely not that old geezer." He rushed off toward the big house.

"Rudy! Wink!" Black Bean Ray ran toward their shack.

Boon went to his shack and woke up Laudee. Everyone met outside.

"What's the matter?" Rudy asked.

"There's gonna be a death tonight," Boon answered with wide eyes.

Chapter 31

"Where am I?"

The barn was musty and damped—cold.

"In between Heaven and Hell, but closer to Hell. Get up, boy. We have a lot of work to get to." The short, stocky overseer yanked on the thick chain connected to the shackle around Tondey's neck, prompting him to get up. Releasing the chain, the overseer tossed him some clothes. "Put them on."

With only undergarments on, Tondey put on the shirt and pants that had been given to him and was led out of a barn by the chain. The forceful sun was an immediate eyesore. He flinched to cover his eyes. "What place is this?"

"You're on the Finch Plantation."

"What happened to—" He looked around and saw cotton fields.

The overseer stopped. "C'mon, let me unloose you."

Tondey walked toward him.

"You try to run, you even flinch, and um gonna kill you. I ain't gonna chase you, but you can be sure I'll catch you." He put his hand on the gun that was holstered on his side. "Um'ma shoot you. Kill you dead."

I'm gonna kill her. The words rushed to Tondey's frontal lobe and begged him to mentally revisit *that night.* As the shackle was released from his neck, his brain gave him a crash course of "that night" that was quickly curtailed when Keeps, a short, skinny, brown skin slave walked up.

Keeps smiled. "You need me boss?"

"This ah..." The overseer looked at Tondey. "What's your name, boy?"

"Walt."

"It can't be Walt, we already have one," Keeps said.

The overseer thought. "Let's go with—"

"Tondey. I've been called Tondey before."

"Before. How many names have you had?" Keeps frowned.

"He's a troublemaker, I hear. Been from one plantation to the next. This will be his last till death take him. Put him to work and if he acts up, he'll be strung up."

"We'll get 'im under control, boss. Don't you worry none. C'mon, Ta—what did you say your name was?"

"Tondey."

"Tondey...Tondey. Well, c'mon, Tondey, let's get at it. We have a lot of daylight to work off." Keeps held on to his smile.

Born and raised in Alabama, Walt, the White man, had seen cotton fields before. As a boy, he'd innocently plucked them from burrs and was surprised to learn that his clothes were made from the very thing he held between his fingers and thumb. But working in a cotton field put all innocence into perspective.

Only brief noonday breaks relieved him from the heat and the heavy sacks that hung around his neck and shoulder. Lunch consisted of water and a few pieces of bread during those breaks. Barefoot, he longed for the hog pen that he used to constantly complain about.

When the day ended, Tondey slowly strolled off the field slouched over. He followed other slaves, clueless about what was to be, completely exhausted, in pain, and wanting a bath to relieve the itches that begged to be scratched. His stomach growled for food. His body ached for relief. *I'll be glad to take the hard bed Ms. Lora Dean had us sleeping on.*

"C'mon, you're in the shack with us." Keeps, who always kept a grin on his face, flashed his brown teeth. At the age of forty with a boyish look, he'd grown up on the Finch Plantation and was a model slave. "It's time to have supper, first."

Tondey followed Keeps to a line of slaves where the overseer's helper served small portions of pork meat and bread on tin plates. There was no kitchen to congregate in, no conversations or questions thrown from one person to the next to be answered, argued, or laughed about. Chairs and utensils were obsolete.

Tondey watched and mimicked others who picked up food from their plates with unwashed hands. Food that fell onto their clothes was plucked from their dirty, sweaty garments and shoved into their mouths.

One, two, three, four, adults, two children, and one baby tied to its mama's chest, Tondey mentally counted.

"Hurry up with supper. It'll be daylight in a matter of hours." The overseer crossed his arms and watched as the slaves placed the empty tin plates in a large bucket that sat on a tall wooden table made up of a few pieces of wood that were barely nailed together.

Void of words or comments, the slaves headed to a single shack under the spell of the fading sun, dirty and exhausted from another long workday.

"Hey?" Tondey ran to catch up with Keeps. "Where did you say we were staying?"

"In that shack." He pointed ahead of him. "It houses us all. The children sleep up top, the grown folks rest on the floor."

"The floor?"

Keeps looked at him. "Yeah, the floor. What do you know? We have it better than some. At least we have a floor. I hear some have dirt for floors. It's cool some nights too. Could be better but could be worse."

Everybody always says it could be worse.

That evening while Tondey tried to sleep, the stench from the field, sweat from the heat, and the smell of neglected teeth mixed with disbursed farts. Thankfully, the opened window and door provided coolness as the night slipped into morning.

"Up, up! C'mon, time to get up!"

The slaves dragged themselves to the field at the sound of the overseer's voice. Another day's work had just begun.

Tondey caught up with Keeps. "We're up early, work all day and sleep only a little at night. We get no breaks from this?"

Keeps smiled. "Come Sunday, that's our rest day."

"A day off?"

"Not the whole day. We leave the fields early, put on our best clothes, and have a large plate of food with all the fixings. Then we stand around talking. We used to sing and dance while ol' Duck Head beat on his drum until the Massa says no more."

"Why?"

"Something 'bout somebody using drumbeats for messaging other slaves to meet and run. We don't have the sounds of a drum no more, but we enjoy the time just the same. We clap, use our hands to make music, and we sing. Boy, do we sing."

On that following Sunday, familiar faces gathered, eating, and talking. Children played.

Tondey, who only knew Keeps, walked over to a tree, and sat, thinking, and remembering what once was while singing and clapping went on in the background. He looked at his hands. "Still black. That ain't changed." He thought about Mildred. "Are you dead or alive? I'm not sorry for hitting her." Ms. Lora Dean, that is. "I'll do it again if I get the chance." Unexpected tears grew. He sniffled. "You sold my son and there's no telling what you did with Mildred. Maybe she *was* yours. Sure did have your features. Maybe that's the secret Mildred said she knew. Don't matter none—not now. You sold her. Or had her killed. And my boy. The only child I had, you sold him."

The overseer walked near the crowd. "Night over. Be daylight in hours. Time to take it in." In his usual stance, with crossed arms, he watched the slaves head to the large shack.

Tondey jogged and slowed up beside Keeps who looked at him. "What now?"

"There's another shack over there. It's small, but it's shelter. I haven't seen no one go in or come out. Why?"

A wagon passed them. Keeps followed it with his eyes. "That's why."

A tall-shirtless male slave in his mid-twenties, whose body was the epitome of a well-sculptured black god, jumped down from the wagon. His muscles flexed when he lifted a teenaged female from it and stood her on the ground. He reached back and did the same for an old woman.

"That's Lady Sue. She goes by both, Lady and Sue, so we put 'em together. Lady Sue. She's been here longer than all us slaves. Born here. That's her shack."

"Who's that?" Tondey gestured at a curly haired bright skinned boy who was the last to jump down from the wagon.

Chapter 32

If I can just get a look at his eyes, I'll know. Don't know how, though. The boy appears to be around ten years old. It hasn't been that long since I left Ms. Lora Dean's plantation. Seems like it was just a few months back when Black Bean Ray pulled me off her. He had no right. Not after she sold off my son and his mama. She had no right.

The next day, Tondey stood in the cotton fields wiping sweat from his forehead with the back of his hands. "No man should be doing this work unless they're getting paid for it. No man," he mumbled to himself.

"Standing too long. Get back to work. The whip will be the next thing you hear, boy. Get to it." With arms folded across his chest and legs spread apart, the wide-brimmed hat the overseer wore made him barely visible from the tall stalks of cotton. He watched the field, looking from one end to the other, and could always tell when there was no activity in the field and by whom.

Tondey couldn't see him, but his casually spoken threat was very visible. Recalling the strikes of a whip on his back all too well, Tondey got back to work. "A man should never be beaten by a whi—"

"Owww!"

The boy's back curved inward after the strike of the overseer's whip went across it. The overseer's hard voice followed. "What did I say? Water, bread. You drop 'em, you drink and eat 'em both from the ground! Get to eating!"

Tondey ran, emerging from the cotton fields in time to see the shirtless curly-headed boy on his hands and knees, holding mud-filled bread.

WHACK! "Eat it, boy!"

"But it's full of dirt."

SMACK!

"ARGH!" he mourned in anguish while stuffing the wet dirty bread in his mouth. Frowning, he chewed and swallowed the hard lump.

"The water too. Drink!"

"Ain't no water. It's in the ground."

"Put your mouth to the ground and suck it up before it's all gone in the dirt!" *WHACK!*

"Ow!" Bending to the ground, the boy sucked up more mud than water.

Gazing so hard at the boy, Tondey never saw the overseer's whip come at him. *SMACK!* "ARGH!"

"Didn't I tell you the next sound you'd hear would be my whip? Get back to the field."

Looking at the boy once more while carrying the large sack, Tondey slowly walked back to his place in the field while rubbing this stinging shoulder.

The overseer's attention returned to the boy. "Because of your clumsiness, there won't be a water break today. Gone. Get, before you don't have a back left to beat."

Walt ran off.

"I swear that boy's the clumsiest I've ever seen." He turned to his helper, a young White man in his early twenties, and motioned at him with the whip. "C'mere."

The helper ran to him. "Yeah!"

"See what you can save."

The helper gathered what bread he could from the ground. Thinking about the slave girl in the field who he had a crush on, he tried to free the bread from as much dirt as possible. He put the wet dirty bread back on the wooden platter and placed it on the poorly made wooden table.

"Lunch time!" the young man yelled. His eyes searched for the slave girl he liked.

The slaves came from the field, some walking slowly, others in a hurry to get the wetness of water down their dry throats. A couple of the guys started to talk to each other.

"Keep it moving. No need for conversating," the overseer said.

The slave girl cut her eyes to the right and smiled at the young White man who exchanged the sentiment.

"There's nothing but bread here and it doesn't take all day to eat it. Hurry up. Eat and get back to the field," the overseer said.

"No water, sir?" the slave man in the front of the line asked.

The overseer answered, "No. That clumsy Walt spilled it again. No time to waste. Get your bread and get to the field. The day is still long and so is the work."

When the day ended, Lady Sue stood waiting to serve the evening bread, meat, and water, which was her regular duty when she wasn't being lent out to another plantation. With skin clinging to her narrow bones, she wore her usual toothless grin as the slaves walked up to get their servings. Young Walt stood next to her. She bent over and whispered in his ear. He looked at her, they smiled at each other, and he ran off toward the big house.

Tondey looked on in disappointment. Once again, he wouldn't be able to get a closer look at the child.

After eating, Tondey caught up with Keeps. "Hey?"

"What'd'ya wanna know this time?"

"That boy, who's his mama?"

"Who, Walt?"

Tondey smiled at the thought that young Walt's name may have originated with his name. "Yeah, Walt."

"You said before that your name was Walt. Was it? Where did you come up with that name?"

"I—um, I heard the name on another plantation. Thought it was different. I liked it. Thought I'd take a go at it."

"A name doesn't matter much to slaves unless we're named by our ma and pa. I guess it would be alright to give yourself a name."

Again, Tondey thought of his namesake and smiled. "Yeah, it's special if it comes from our own family."

"Walt, the massa just up and bring him one day. He's been here since he was a baby. He gave him to Lady Sue to give her something to do. Somebody to take care of."

"Why's she so special?"

"Lady Sue? She was his friend when they were young. She had a husband who died years back. That left her sad for a while. The massa gave her Walt to make her feel better."

"They said where the boy came from? Before he came here?"

"From Virginia, I hear. Why?"

"Just wondering." *Virginia.* Tondey walked slower, allowing Keeps to walk ahead of him. *It's him. He's my boy. Then, how long have I been gone and where have I been in all that time?*

Chapter 33

The clammy, musky room had become the norm for those who all lay on the wooden floor. But that night, Tondey found it hard to sleep after learning that Walt might be his son. He sat up in the dark, barely able to see.

The sounds of snoring spoke loudly. "What'd'ya want, old man." His whisper was barely audible. "Why're you sitting in that corner staring at me? What do you have stewing up now? Every time you come, something bad happens. You done brought me here and made me a slave. Since that time, they've cut off my manhood and sold my only child. They've beat me and sold me off. Now, you have me jumping from one place to different times. What do you want from me now? Ain't nothing left to learn. Nothing but more pain."

The old man's face was motionless. The moment Tondey blinked, he was gone.

That morning, Tondey dragged himself to the field after getting only a couple of hours of sleep. He was worried. *When he comes, something happens. Most times bad.*

That morning, the weather was so pleasant that the slaves didn't mind working so much until the sun started burning.

The overseer yelled, "Break time. Come get your bread and water. C'mon. No lagging, gagging around—let's go!"

Tondey's hope to see Walt was satisfied the moment he arrived, carrying a large platter of bread that was pressed against his chest while lugging a huge wooden jug of water at his side. The child was fearfully focused.

"Break time!" the overseer's helper reminded them.

The slaves emerged from the field and made their way to the wooden table where Walt was placing the platter of bread. He struggled to lift the heavy jug of water.

Tondey broke from the line and ran to help him. "OW!" The overseer's whip slapped his shoulder.

"Get back in line, boy! The only thing that teaches him is this here whip. Let him be taught."

Tondey rubbed his shoulder with brewing anger while he walked back to the line.

Walt struggled to hold on to the jug that slipped from his fingers and landed upright on the ground. Before retrieving it, he made sure he had a tighter grip on the platter. He stooped low and blindly felt for it. "Got it." Another sting from the whip made him knock over the jug. It fell on its side and seeped out water.

Walt set the platter of bread on the ground and went to pick up the jug. The overseer's whip came across his hand. He grunted. Tears built up in his eyes as he rubbed his hand. The overseer hit him again, making the ten-year-old cry.

A few slaves motioned to help him.

"Not one of you move. He has to learn. You keep crying, boy, and um'ma give you a reason to. Hurry up, you high yellow rodent." He pulled the whip back and took it up to strike Walt again but was stopped. He looked behind him and saw Tondey towering and tightly gripping his raised wrist.

The helper ran over to stop Tondey but received a hard elbow to his nose. He dropped to the ground.

"Boy, you done did it now." Anger was on the overseer's face. "You let go this minute."

"Not if you gonna keep hitting the boy."

The overseer scoffed. "You have some nerve to order me. No, I'm not gonna strike the boy with it. Not him."

His crazed wide-eyed stare made Tondey aware of the sacrifice he'd made. Releasing the overseer's wrist, he stepped back with raised hands and was quickly wrestled to the ground by the helper who'd gotten up and grabbed him from behind. The overseer joined in on the take-down.

That night, Tondey was sliced so many times by the whip's wand, that blood dripped out of him like a running faucet. "Paty. I need Paty," he mourned when seeing Keeps and the well-toned slave who had come to unstrap him from the apparatus that was used to hang and whip slaves.

"Who's Paty?" the well-toned slave asked Keeps.

Tondey tried to raise his dangling head. He looked around as much as he could to see that they were the only two there. "Where's everybod—?"

"Sleeping. Overseer came knocking. Said for us to take you down."

"Where's the boy? Where's Walt?"

They wrapped Tondey's arms around their necks and dragged him to the shack.

Lady Sue held the door open and pointed. "Lay 'im right there."

They laid him on the floor on top of the blankets she had ready for him.

"Turn 'im on his side and prop him there to keep them wounds from sticking to the blanket." She walked over and took a closer look at the cuts. "Yeah, he got the whip in the worst way. Overseer tried to kill him."

Chapter 34

"He's awake, Ma'am." With crossed legs, elbows resting on them and his hands to his cheeks, Walt sat directly in front of Tondey who was still propped on his side.

Tondey opened his eyes to see the most beautiful pair of green eyes staring back. "It's you. It's—you're my son. My boy, it's you."

"What's he's saying?" Lady Sue asked.

"Something about his boy."

Still in pain, Tondey smiled and mumbled. "It's you."

Lady Sue walked over to him. "Let me take a look at you." The itsy-bitsy aged woman knelt to the floor and rested on one knee. "You're as dark as me." Taking his shoulder, she pulled him toward her and leaned over to look at his back, touching it. "Mmhmm..." Leaning him back on his side, she patted his arm and got up from the floor. "It's gonna heal. It'll just be a minute, but your back will close after a while. You saved Walt from the whip. Um gonna take real good care of you 'cause you did that. C'mon, let's get you up. I have to get some food in your stomach."

After propping him in a sitting position with Walt's help, she sat on the floor, crossed her thin legs, and fed him from a plate of peas and some sort of meat.

Tondey smiled.

"What're you smiling for?" she asked.

"You remind me of somebody I loved. Paty, from the sickhouse."

"Who's this Paty, your wife?"

"No...but I wanted her. I always kept that to myself. I never told anyone. Back then, I was blind with foolish hatred."

"Hatred? Who do you hate, the massa?" Walt asked.

He looked at Walt and smiled. "No...I think it was knowledge. I think it was truth."

"What truth is that?"

Walt's little curious mind made Tondey instantly fall in love with him. He grinned. "That the White man hates the Black man for no-good reason. That the White man did more to the Black man than the Black man did to the White man. The White man gave the Black man plenty reasons to hate 'em. Instead, they forgave us."

"Who is us?"

"That's the pain talking. I meant *we* forgave the White man who still wanna hold *us* back for no good reason. For no-good reason, we, *I mean*, they, the White man, hate the Black man for no-good reason." With a solemn stare, Tondey's eyes filled with water. "Hate 'em for no-good reason."

"Are you about to cry?"

"Walt, leave the man alone. Let 'em eat." Lady Sue scooped another pile of peas and took it to Tondey's mouth.

Looking at the two of them, he felt a warm feeling inside that made him smile. He opened his mouth and took the food she fed him.

Over the next two weeks, Tondey constantly gleamed with joy while watching Walt sit, eat, and sleep, and engage him with many questions.

Lady Sue convinced the overseer that she needed Walt's help with Tondey. "He can barely sit up and um a little lady. I need Walt's help with 'im. And when I tend to supper, I need Walt to mind 'im for me 'cause he's been beaten so bad, he needs minding."

"Like hell he does. I need Walt in the field to get bread and water and other things."

"This is more important. We're caring for a man you done beat near death. A few days missing a child won't stop slaves from working the fields. When Tondey's well enough, I'll get Walt to the field myself."

"Walt will be in the field every day, working like every other slave on this plantation. Um the overseer. I oversee the slaves, not you."

"I need to get massa to say so?"

With tensed lips, the overseer barely opened his mouth while speaking. "Gone get, you old bat. But I want 'im back to work in two weeks. I can't have lazy niggers on this plantation."

Lady Sue started walking toward the kitchen house to help prepare the evening feed for the slaves once they left the fields. She stopped. "Why do you hate us?"

"What?"

"You heard me. Why do you hate us Black folks?"

"'Cause...'cause...I don't owe you no reason."

"'Cause it's a no-good reason, that's why."

"What? What're you talking about."

"That reason for you hating us. It's a no-good reason. That's what it is. No good." With a lifted nose and revulsion upon her face, she walked away.

"I don't need a good reason, you old bat!"

She continued walking.

His words got louder. "I don't owe you a reason! You're lucky the massa lay-up with you years back. You're lucky you're old. If he didn't protect you, I'd feed you to the dogs for talking to me like that!" He scoffed and headed for the fields. "Old bat. I'm gonna lend her off for talking to me like that. As soon as the massa's gone, um gonna lend her off again. Old black bat."

~~~~~

While helping Tondey put on a shirt, Walt noticed the whip marks on his back. "You have new and old scars. You've been beaten before?"

"Yeah. Um no stranger to the whip."

"They like to hurt us." Walt's face grew gloomy. "Not just the whip. They hurt us other ways too."

"What do you mean, *other ways*?"

Walt dropped his head. "The overseer, he hurts me in other ways."

"How?"

They turned to see Lady Sue walking in. "The workday was long but gone. What are y'all up to? Walt, you'll be staying with in Tondey 'til he's ready for the field."

"The overseer won't let me."

"I've already taken care of that. You'll stay. Here, I have y'all some supper. Not that mess they feed the field slaves. I have some leftovers from massa's supper."

That night, they ate well. By then, Tondey was able to feed himself. And the bed pallet he slept on while with Lady Sue was more comfortable than the hard floor he had to share with seven other slaves. The herbs Lady Sue gave him helped him to sleep soundly, even through the knock that came to the door one late evening.

Lady Sue answered. "What do you want?"

"I need the boy to help me with something."

She looked the overseer over. Looking at the wide-brimmed hat he always wore and his lack of hygiene, she frowned. "What do you need 'im for? He's asleep."

Rubbing his eyes, Walt sat up.

The overseer looked around her at Walt. "Not anymore. C'mere, boy. I need your help."

Walt looked at Lady Sue.

"How long do you need 'im for? The boy needs his sleep like everybody else."

"Not long. I have some wood needing stacked. I'll send 'im right back after we're done."

She turned to Walt and nodded.

He slowly got up and walked out the door, looking back at her as the overseer put his hand to his back.

"I'll have 'im back shortly. Not much to do, but it has to be done just the same."

~~~~~

"Gone in." With his hand to Walt's back, the overseer pushed Walt toward the door of his one-room shack.

"I'on wanna go in."

"Boy, I said get."

Walt lowered his head and slowly walked in. He turned around to see the overseer closing the door. Tears began falling. "I wanna go to Lady Sue."

"You will. Right after. Gone, drop 'em."

"I'on wanna."

"Boy, drop 'em. I need to get the whip?"

"I'on wanna." Walt rubbed tears from his eyes.

The overseer went to the corner of the room where he'd thrown the whip earlier.

"Please don't," Walt wept. "Please."

"Drop 'em, boy." He held the whip out front. "You gonna get this to your back and um gonna make you drop 'em just the same."

"Please, don't. I'on wanna. I wanna go back to Lady Sue. Please. I wanna go back to Lady Sue." Tears continued releasing. So many fell from his eyes as he untied his pants and held them.

"Gone, finish."

"Please, I wanna go back to Lady Sue." Walt wiped tears with the back of his hands while releasing his pants. They slipped down to his ankles.

"Turn around."

"Please, don't." Walt slowly turned with just his shirt on.

"You know what to do."

Still weeping, Walt bent over.

The overseer walked up behind him and pulled down his pants. He put his hand on Walt's back while the child cried. "Remember, you tell and um gonna sell you and kill the old lady."

The sound of Walt's cries grew louder.

~~~~~

Walt returned to the shack.

Lady Sue held the door for him. "I fixed your bed back up. Made it comfortable for you. Gone get in it."

With a dropped head, Walt climbed in.

"Walt, are you all right?"

"Yeah." He lay down.

Chapter 35

Tondey stood shirtless with his back to Lady Sue.

"Yeah, it's better," she said. "Not all the way healed, but a couple more days and you'll be well enough for the field."

"If he goes to the field, that means I have to work too." Walt crossed his arms over his chest and pouted.

"What, you don't like working?" Tondey slipped his shirt over his head and pulled it down.

"I'on mind working. It's just that the overseer, he likes beating us niggers. And when the others be in the field, um the closest, so he beats me. I'on like 'im. He beats me. And..." He dropped his head."

"And what?"

He looked at Tondey. "And he hates me...us, for no-good reason, he hates us."

"C'mere."

Walt walked into Tondey's arms that wrapped him close and held him tight. He placed the side of his face on Tondey's stomach then looked up at him. His green eyes were full of water. "I wish I could stay here forever. I feel safe right here."

"Yeah, I wish you could too. It makes no sense to take hatred out on a child." Taking Walt's arms, Tondey knelt on one knee in front of him. "If he hits you, he'll have to hit me too. I won't let 'im beat you. I'll protect you."

Lady Sue took a step closer to Tondey to get his attention. "But if you try to stop 'im, he'll kill you for sure next time, you know."

Turning from her, he looked directly into Walt's green eyes. "Some things are worth dying for." Still on one knee, he pulled the boy in and wrapped him into his dark-skin hug.

The next day, Lady Sue checked Tondey's back again. "Yep, you're healed for sure. I'll let the overseer know to give you another day. I have to get to the kitchen. Help get supper ready for the slaves when they leave the field." Unlatching the door, she left.

Tondey looked at Walt and smiled. Knowing that the time left with him would be short, he grabbed him and rubbed his black curly hair. He wanted to enjoy every moment as if it would be his last.

He shared everything he could think of with his son. "This is how you can tell the north from the south... Did you know some trees and plants are poison and some have fruits or roots good for eating?"

"No. Which ones?"

"Good question. Some you can eat, but others, you can't. If there's milky white sap or..."

The new information fascinated Walt and kept him asking questions.

"Hey, um..." Looking at Walt, Tondey wondered if he should ask the question that had been burning at him since he left Ms. Lora

Dean's plantation. He rubbed his dark lips and pushed the question between them. "What do you know about your ma?"

"My ma? That's Lady Sue. She's my ma."

"And she's a good ma too." He grabbed Walt, wrestled, and played with him.

Walt wrestled to get away but was caught by Tondey who pulled him from behind. "No, please." Walt snatched loose.

"Um just playing with you." Tondey touched Walt's shoulder and a terrified little boy turned around to face him. "Walt, um not gonna hurt you. I'll never do anything to hurt you. You're my bb...Why are you so scared of me?"

"'Cause ..." Walt dropped his head.

"'Cause what?"

"It's the overseer. He does things to hurt me. Makes me do things to him too."

A feeling Tondey had never had before washed over him. An uncontrollable, untamed emotion that burned from within, causing him to feel feverish. He looked down at Walt, who looked up with his green eyes. Tondey's eyes grew monstrous, scaring Walt.

"Um, sorry. I didn't mean to—"

"C'mere, son." Tondey gripped his son in a bear hug. He released him so the tight grip wouldn't hurt him and hurriedly left the small shack, growling like an angry lion. With the overseer in his sights, he ran as fast as he could toward the cotton field. The overseer stood idly, legs spread apart, arms folded across his chest, and wearing his wide-brimmed hat. Rushing him, Tondey lifted and threw him on the ground. Angry blows to the overseer's face left Tondey's fists bleeding. It took the strength of the two strongest slaves and the overseer's helper to pull the feral Tondey off the overseer.

With swollen jaws, busted lips, and nearly closed eyes, the overseer stood, but struggled. He felt his nose. "I'll kill 'im. Um gonna kill that nigger. He broke my damn nose. Um gon' kill that nigger. Um'ma kill—" Barely able to stand, he looked at his helper. "Go get Pete from the Plackley Plantation. Tell 'im I sent for 'im. Boy, um gonna string you up and skin you alive. You're gonna beg me for death."

The overseer's helper released Tondey to the two slaves, jumped on his horse and rushed off.

That evening, Lady Sue sat on the floor with an inconsolable Walt on her lap. Hearing a knock on the door, she tried to lift Walt off her lap, but he wouldn't budge.

"Lady Sue, it's me, Keeps. Open up."

"Walt, I need to get the door."

He sat up with a face full of tears.

She opened the door to Keeps and the well-toned slave. "How is he?"

Keeps shook his head. "He's still living...barely. The overseer wanted to hang 'im, but the massa, he said he wants his investment back. So, they're selling 'im. A man loaded 'im on his wagon. He's talking to the massa in the house. Tondey's on the back of the wagon. He asked for Walt."

Hearing the conversation, Walt burst out of the shack just as the wagon drove away. "Tondey! Tondey! Tondey!"

Severely beaten, hands tied behind his back, a chain collared around his neck, Tondey attempted to rise up, but the shaky wagon and restraints denied him. He fell over on his side, gazed up at the dark sky and stars, and wept as his son's cries faded.

Chapter 36

Twice, Tondey had been beaten after attacking a White person. Each time, it had been for the sake of his son. *I had to protect him from the White man's hatred.* However, each time, his fast fists caused him to lose him. And at the age of forty-nine, Tondey wondered if he'd ever see Walt again.

He sat on the floor beneath a stairway, a closet that was used as his space, where he slept with two blankets. One to lay on, one to cover with.

"Tondey, get in here! I need you." The voice was soft but stern.

"Yes, ma'am, um coming." He limped to a bedroom.

"Gimme that bottle over there." The missus of Sheriff Tuck rested her back against a large, beautiful washtub. It had been given to her as a wedding gift.

"Which bottle, ma'am?"

"That one, boy. You stupid or something? There's only three on the bureau."

Tondey looked at all three bottles and made a choice. Picking up the larger one, he limped it over to her.

"That's not it—the other one."

He limped back, chose the shorter one, and took it to her.

"Boy, I swear, you have to be dumber than the chicken you tend to." She stood, completely naked with bushy pubic hairs showing and all. "What're you looking for? You can't have it. Couldn't even if I gave it to you." Stepping out of the tub, she went to the shelf, snatched the only bottle Tondey hadn't grabbed, and shoved it in his face. "You see this—this is what I was asking for." Walking back to the tub, she climbed in. "I don't know why God wasted brains on niggers."

Tondey turned to leave the room.

"Where are you going?"

"If that's all, ma'am, I'll let you get back to your wash."

"You get back here."

He turned to face her.

"Get that jug I asked you to fill earlier. I need you to rinse my hair after I wash it." Looking at the bottle she'd taken from the shelf, she read it. "My grandmother's friend gave me this stuff as a wedding gift." She dipped her fingers in the jar and lifted a thick light pink paste-like substance. "Here, put it back over there."

Tondey did as she told, then waited, watching the wall he faced.

The missus rubbed the substance in the palms of her hands and massaged it into her hair. "Hey, come wash my hair."

Tondey walked over.

She leaned back as he massaged the shampoo through her hair. "Ooh-wee, this stuff stinks. Get it out, hurry up, get it out. Seems like the more you massage it in, the stinkier it gets. Get it out!"

Moving as fast as he could, Tondey picked up the heavy jug and poured.

She sat up and leaned forward. "Pour it slowly, boy."

Feeling its weight growing the longer he held it, he poured faster.

"Did I say faster? I won't be rushed by you. Whew, this stink. Pour slower! Rinse, nigger, rinse."

~~~~~

Days later...

"Nigger!"

Tondey rested in a corner of the closet beneath the staircase, eyes closed, back to a wall. His hands rested on his knees.

"Nigger!"

Disgusted by the word he had used on numerous occasions when he lived as Walt in his former life, Tondey shook his head in shame.

"Nigger! Get in here."

"I know I better answer," he said to the old man who sat on the opposite side of the small tight space. He had long since stopped fussing at him. In fact, he'd come to appreciate the old man's visits. Especially while enslaved by the sheriff and his wife. He was their only servant and was often alone with only chores to keep him company.

The sheriff worked all day and was out all night with friends, men, and women alike. Tondey had very little interaction with him. The sheriff's wife, however, was a constant posturing presence who always seemed to need him to do something, no matter the hour, day, or night.

"Nigger! Get in here right now!"

Tondey stood and straightened his thin pants that were barely holding together by threads. Dragging his weakened leg, he stopped next to the old man and looked down at him.

The old man kept staring at the corner as if Tondey was still there.

"Hmp. I can touch you to see if you're real or just in my mind. I'd rather fool myself that you are." He looked up and continued walking, following the sound of the missus' voice that led him upstairs to her bedroom.

"Nigger!"

He knocked.

"Get in here!"

He slowly opened the door.

"Give me that brush."

Tondey looked at the brush that was an arm's reach away from where she sat in front of the vanity. He picked it up and held it out to her.

"Why are you giving it to me? Brush."

Positioning himself behind her, he applied long fast strokes down her brownish straight hair.

"You know I hate niggers. Hate 'em, I tell you. Their dark skin...and they smell. I can't stand the way they smell. Even the lighter ones. I hate them even more. Trying to be all proper when they're fit for nothing but stepping and spitting on."

Why?

As if she'd read his thoughts, she continued. "I don't need a reason, I just don't like 'em. But I have one. I have a real reason. I'm just not telling it to you. I don't have to tell it. But it's why I'm not sitting in some big house, married to some slave owner or some powerful man."

What is she talking about?

"I'm talking about what niggers have taken from me. I hate 'em, I do." She looked in the mirror, and seeing Tondey, she frowned. "I hate you too. You're the darkest nigger I've ever seen. And you are here, in my house, serving me. You're my nigger. My own personal slave, given to me as a gift by my grandfather. You know what nigger?"

He kept brushing. *What?*

Grabbing a glass of wine that sat on her vanity next to a half-filled decanter, she took a sip then looked at him in the mirror again. "I have a secret, you know. Just my grandfather and me." She drank the last of the wine from the glass, poured more, drank, and set the glass down.

What's with these White folks and their secrets?

"It's our secret. The reason I'm..." Rapidly shaking her head from side to side, she threw her face in her hands.

The long, fast strokes of the brush slowed. He eased the brush's bristles along the roots of her scalp, allowing them to massage with every slow stroke.

She leisurely dropped her arms, raised her head, and stared at her sad reflection in the mirror. After a while, her eyes became heavy. Blinking them sluggishly, a single tear released.

Seeing the sleepiness in her eyes, Tondey stopped brushing and stepped to her side. "Ma'am, let me get you to the bed."

Sighing softly, she stood.

He laid the brush on the vanity and took her by the elbow. He placed another hand on her back and guided her to the bed. Once in her room, she turned and looked at him. "You niggers are good for something, aren't you? Gone...get, so I can relieve myself of my attire."

His eyes widened. I helped you relaxed, and you still call me nigger?

Chapter 37

Oftentimes, Tondey caught glimpses of the missus' sadness peeking from beyond her resting face. Once he stood staring, watching as she looked in the mirror with tears drizzling down her face. Lifting her eyes from her reflection, they landed on him. He rushed away but was caught by her voice. "Nigger! Why are you standing around with idle hands? Go clean something!"

Tondey remembered working with hogs and pulling cotton, but being so dark, he never imagined that he would be a domesticated slave. He learned that although he wasn't in the field, "Boon and Mawbee were right. We're still all slaves, being slaved."

"It's about time you learned how to cook. You can't keep eating my good cooking. You're the slave, not me," The missus said while walking toward the kitchen doorway. She stopped, turned around, and looked at him. "C'mon, nigger. It's time for you to learn how to cook."

The task of learning how to cook was challenging for him. No matter how hard she tried, he just couldn't get it. At least that's what he was letting on.

"I can't teach you to count measurements, 'cause you niggers are too dumb to learn arithmetic. I can't write down the measurements for you to read, because you're too dumb to learn to read and write. You're just one worthless nigger. Worthless, I tell you."

I can read. I'm just not letting you know I can. Why do I have to learn to feed you good food when all I get is the leftovers and scraps from your plate like um a stray dog?

When there were leftovers, he'd often scrape what he could from the pot before cleaning it. Sometimes it was enough to comfort his hungry stomach, oftentimes it wasn't. But there was no weight to lose from the skinny man that he had become.

Tondey was company to the missus, but not the one she desired. That person was her husband, and the moment the sheriff stayed home a full night and was there the following morning, she took her frustration of loneliness out on him. "You're never home. I'm home all alone with this DUMB nigger. He can't cook, he can't clean, and he limps. I need a girl who can do all those things."

"You want me to sell the nigger? Trade him for a female slave?"

"No. He's good with farming and gardening but he's no domesticated slave. He's smut black for Heaven's sake. Dark slaves were never meant to be good house slaves."

Smut black. Tondey recalled using those words all the time. He remembered hearing his mother and auntie using them. *It had to have been passed down from back this far.*

"You would know," the sheriff said to his wife. The harsh, familiar words had made their way back into an uncomfortable conversation.

Stunned by their sting, the missus ignored them. "Husband, I need help, can't you understand? I wasn't raised to cook and clean. We had servants. Slaves to do laundry, to draw my baths, to—to—"

"You are a slave, Jenny Bell. You're as Black as our servant, Tondey. No man of honor would ever marry you. I only did so for power. And, of course, to relieve your grandfather of his shame. He begged me to take you off his hands."

"It's not my fault, Husband. It's not my fault. It's my mother's sin that I must bear. And no one in this town knows. No one but you. Must you burden every conversation we have with her sin? I'm your wife."

"No! You're my problem. You were your grandfather's humiliation, now I carry his plight."

With a dropped head, Jenny Bell's eyes welled with tears. "If you'll just give me a child, a baby to love, I won't be so lonely." She raised her head, so he could witness the pain in her watery eyes.

"Ha! Me? Give you a child and have nigger blood running through the veins of my seed? Never. I married you for power, Jenny Bell, nothing more. Your grandfather couldn't push you off on anyone, so he begged the favor of me in exchange for the mayor's seat. And as soon as it's time to vote our current mayor out of office, I'll be ready to step in his stead. All I need you to do is play the part of a dutiful wife. And with that role will come power, money, and the help you're pleading for."

"I'll tell grandfather, I will. I'll tell him that you've been everything but a husband to me. That you refuse to bed me after our wedding night to consummate our union. That you—"

"Do you think he cares what goes on in our bedroom?"

"I was—am—my grandfather's favorite. My happiness is his concern. And I shall tell him of your conduct toward your wife."

He held her eyes in his view with sadistic smile. "Very well."

Thinking she'd gotten her way, she smiled.

He did the same. "Tell him. See if I care. Or better yet, learn that he doesn't."

Chapter 38

A month later...

Jenny Bell hurried around the kitchen, cooking a big meal of what she'd assumed was all her husband's favorites. When she'd served him that meal before, it was the only time he'd closed his eyes and bounced his head as if he was enjoying it.

Walking to the four-seater table, she carefully placed a crystal pie dome on it. "There." She smiled. "You always knew how proud I was about my pies, grandmother. Thank you for the lovely wedding gift."

Tondey walked in. "Is that a pie?"

"Yes. My secret recipe. An apple pie. I call it, *Jenny Bell's Heaven*." She looked at him. "I suppose if there's any left, you may have a taste. I do enjoy watching the look of pure enjoyment on the faces of those who taste my pie."

She leaned toward him. "Truth be told, it's the recipe of my grandfather's cook, whose name was Pearl. I lived in her kitchen as a child. Me being there would drive grandfather *crazy*. He would hasten me out the moment he got wind that I was there. But whenever he was away, I'd sneak into the kitchen and Pearl would allow me to help her cook. Thankfully."

Her face grew weary. "Who knew that I would be a domesticated wife? A woman of my grandfather's wealth would marry some commoner, some local poor, power-hungry sheriff with his eyes on the seat of a good mayor." She pulled a chair from beneath the table and flopped in it.

Tondey walked near her and began massaging her head. She shrugged him. "Go find some work to do before I do so for you, nigger."

Dropping his head, he walked away.

A few hours later, her husband came in. "I chopped enough wood to get you through half of this winter."

"Why chop wood when we have Tondey? And why only for me and not for us? This is our home, husband, not mine alone—"

"Chopping wood helps me to stay in shape for the ladies, Jenny Bell."

She dropped her head.

"I have to go get cleaned up."

"Yes, please, to prepare for dinner. I cooked you the most scrumptious meal. And a few days back, I went into town and purchased a nice, expensive brandy."

"I'm going into town tonight. I won't be back for a couple of days. I have to prepare for the mayor's race coming up next year."

"Husband, please. Grant me this one evening to feed you before you head out."

He dropped his shoulders on his way to the door, then stopped. "I suppose I could grant you this one evening." He glanced back at her and smiled. "You are a good wife, Jenny Bell." He walked away.

That evening, they ate in silence. He drank more brandy than he consumed food. She assured that by instructing Tondey earlier to, "Make sure his glass stays full."

With a plate half full of food, Sheriff Tuck could barely sit without leaning.

"Tondey?" Taking the napkin from her lap, the missus stood. "Please help my husband to bed."

Tondey lifted the sheriff.

The sheriff looked at Tondey. "Where're you taking me?"

Jenny Bell answered. "To bed, my dear husband. He's taking you to bed."

"But I have to leave for town. She'll be waiting for me."

Not tonight, husband. She waved for Tondey to take him.

Tondey walked him away.

"Oh, Tondey?" she called.

The sheriff was heavy. The thin, older Tondey could barely bear him. He stopped and turned to her with the sheriff's arm still across his shoulder. "Yes, ma'am," he grunted.

"Undress him. Make him completely nude."

Although the sheriff's body was heavy, Tondey couldn't help but look at her a moment longer. He knew that the expensive brandy she'd bragged about had been meant to knock the sheriff out.

He turned and walked the sheriff to their bedroom, undressed and put him to bed, then returned to the dining room where the missus stood holding a plate of apple pie and a dessert folk that she held out to him. "After cutting the turkey and bringing in the vegetables from the garden, I suppose you deserve this. Here."

Tondey was slow to receive her offering.

"It's all right, take it."

He took the pie, leaving her holding the dessert fork. Picking up the slice of pie, he shoved it in his mouth.

She watched the moment his eyes widened.

It's the same pie. I know this pie blindfolded. It's a little richer. I can tell that the ingredients are more authentic, not thinned out by boxed or canned ingredients. He took another bite. *Yep, it's the same pie from my ma's recipe but it's sooo much better. My God, it's so much better.*

"I told you. It's to die for, isn't it?"

"It is, ma'am. Apple pie is my favorite, and it's because of this same recipe."

She smiled. "Well, there's plenty left. I suppose my husband will leave first thing in the morning, and I would prefer it not go to waste. Clean up and have the leftovers. There's plenty."

"Yes, ma'am."

She left and headed directly for their bedroom.

Tondey sat at the table looking at the pie displayed under the crystal pie dome. He stuck out his arm and observed the color of his dark skin. He recalled the night he tried to run over the old man and the glare in the man's eyes the closer his truck got to him. "How was it that I was able to see your eyes in the dark when I was so far away? It was as if I ran right into 'em, destined to see what you needed to show me." He stood and started cleaning up. "Destined to see what you're showing me now. There was and still is so much to learn, isn't there?"

Chapter 39

Sheriff Tuck was up and gone before the sun came out.

The missus arose, got dressed, and headed to the kitchen to prepare food like she did every morning. She always cooked just a little too much in order to leave enough scraps for Tondey. Humming while walking around the house, she found things for Tondey to clean once and twice again.

She's happier than normal. Ain't no sign of sadness nowhere on her face. The thought that she would remain that way was refreshing but Tondey knew all too well the reason for her joy that he knew wouldn't last.

Later that day. "Tondey?"

Hearing her call, he went upstairs to her bedroom. "Yes, ma'am."

"Make me laugh, Tondey. Entertain me."

"Like what, ma'am? What do you want me to do?"

"I don't know, dance, tell a joke, sing, do something." Looking in the mirror, she laid a pearl necklace against her chest. "Nooo, maybe, this one." She picked out another necklace to test against her dress.

He looked down and thought. Jenny Bell didn't pay him any attention while he considered how to entertain her. His favorite song came to mind. Tondey opened his mouth and let out a beautiful baritone. "Lady...You're my night and shining armor...and I love you," he sang.

Dangling a necklace against her chest, the missus stopped and looked in the mirror at Tondey. She turned in her seat. Crossing her leg, she gave him her full attention.

He continued, "You have made me what I am andddd...I am yours..."

Swelling tears fell down her face. She took a handkerchief and wiped them away. By the time he'd finished, the cloth was wet. She sniffed. "I've never heard anyone sing that way before. Where did you learn that song from?"

"From a guy named Kenny Rogers. A White man, ma'am."

"You have the most amazing voice. Have you always sung that way?"

Thinking about his former life when he was Walt, he recalled the first time he heard a Black boy singing in school. His childhood friend, Roy, remarked, "Black people have three good talents, running, dancing, and singing. Walt, I guess you're Black, because you can sing too."

Little did Roy know. It was funny when Roy had said it, but standing in front of her, it was all making sense that he'd gotten his talent *from me. From Tondey.*

~~~~~

The first month, she glowed with joy, *but I can't celebrate too soon. After all, I've been late a few times before.* By the second month, she could barely contain the delight that always stretched across her face.

The few times the sheriff was home, he even noticed that she didn't complain. "Are you alright, Jenny Bell?" the sheriff said one late afternoon.

"I'm wonderfully happy, my dear husband."

"I'm glad for you, Jenny. There's something new about you. Something quite appealing. You're glowing. It's quite ravishing really." He had no idea that by that time; she was four months pregnant. "And quite fetching, I might add."

Staring at each other, the two raced to the other's arms. He tried ripping her clothes off, but the quality of the well-sown fabric and thread made it impossible. He turned her back to him, lifted her dress, and ripped off her undergarments. Bending her over, he took her from behind. Three minutes later he backed away from her. "Goodness..." He buttoned his pants while she turned to face him. "You were a virgin. I suppose I never thought about it. Did I hurt you?"

"No. It was perfect, husband. It was everything I'd hope it would be," she lied and climbed into bed.

Two months later, her six-month-old belly was quite plump.

The sheriff wasn't happy about her pregnancy but preparing for the campaign of a lifetime kept him away a lot. Or so he claimed that to be the reason. When he was finally home for a few days in a row, she sat him down and stated the obvious. "Dear husband, I'm with child. We're going to have a baby."

"No, Jenny Bell, you're going to have a baby...alone."

"Whatever do you mean? I'm pregnant with your—"

"I've told you I will not be the father to a child who has the blood of a slave. A nigger. And frankly, while we're on the topic, why is it that your belly is twice the size it should be? We had sex only a couple of months ago. Surely your stomach shouldn't have grown that much in size two months later. Did you grow so desperate that you bedded Tondey?"

"Oh, my word. Husband, how can you accuse me of such a foul act? I've only been with you. The child in my stomach belongs to my husband."

"Am I to believe that after bedding you two months ago, your stomach has grown that hastily? I will not be made a fool of, Jenny Bell. If you have not allowed Tondey to bed you...Oh, I dare not even think of it without shame. The very thought of you bringing dishonor to my good name by being with another man infuriates me. Is this the way you chose to repay my kindness to your grandfather?"

"Husband, please, I...I hate the skin of a Black man, I tell you. No matter his color. I hate the Black blood that runs through my veins. And I have never been with another. Not before you, nor have I after our marriage. A child from my *White* husband would further suppress the curse my mother has given me. My child, *our child*, will be White as snow. Only a very, small fraction of Black blood would remain in its vein. We shall raise it to hate the Black man as I do. As we do. To take its rightful place in this world, receiving all the privileges of a White person."

Beholding her pregnant state, he was silent for a moment. "I will have no part of it, nor you. I will only allow you to be by my side as my lawful wife while campaigning. In fact, we will use your pregnancy to garner voters' sympathy. A young mayor and his pregnant wife. Yes! But after I have claimed the title of mayor and the power and wealth that comes from such a prestigious position, I will have nothing more to do with you, nor your child. You can remain in our household and play the role of a dutiful wife, but it is the only role that you will have."

Chapter 40

The doctor delivered Jenny Bell's daughter with ease. The moment she held the little human in her arms, she cried tears of joy. "I shall name you Delores, after my dear grandmother."

Cooing, the small child opened her eyes and looked into the face of her smiling mother.

"That's a fine baby girl, Jenny Bell. You and the sheriff should be proud. Speaking of the sheriff, I suppose he's out doing sheriff's business or working on his campaign. If I see him in town today, I'll let him know to get home. He's a father now. I'm sure he will rush to be by your side." The doctor rubbed the baby's head. "She's a fine baby girl...Well, I need to get home to my wife. If you need me, just have the sheriff get word to me."

"I shall. Be well, doctor, and thank you for delivering my precious joy."

"It's the best part of my job. Try to get some rest, Jenny Bell."

"I shall try. Tondey! Tondey!"

Tondey came into the room.

"Please see the doctor out."

"Yes, ma'am." Tondey stuck out a hand, guiding the way for the doctor who followed him.

When Tondey returned, he saw the baby in Jenny Bell's arms and smiled. "May I come in, ma'am?"

"Yes."

The baby started crying.

"Maybe it's hungry. Maybe it's ready to feed?"

"I guess it's time to start my motherly duties. Oh, this is all so new for me. How will I take care of such a small human?"

"Like all mothers before you, ma'am. I think it comes natural."

She smiled. "I suppose so." As she prepared to feed the baby, Tondey rushed to a chair, and taking a blanket from it, he covered her breast as the baby fed.

"It's a boy or girl?"

"A girl." Jenny Bell stared at the baby while feeding her.

"A girl. You have a name for it?"

"Delores."

"That's a pretty name. I went to school with..."

She looked at him for answers.

"I figured I'll make you laugh. I guess I'll leave you to feed her. I'll be back shortly, see if you need me to do anything."

She didn't respond.

Tondey left and returned a couple of hours later with a plate of food, something he threw together. "Ma'am...Sleeping." He placed the food on the table next to the bed and, hearing the baby cooing, walked to the other side. Looking down at the baby girl, he smiled.

Chapter 41

A few days after Jenny Bell had given birth, the doctor saw the sheriff at the market. "How's little Delores?"

"Pardon me."

"Your baby girl, how's she doing? And Jenny Bell? It's been three days since she delivered."

"Oh, yeah. They're swell, doctor. They're doing just fine. I'm, uh, I'm here at the market to get some things Jenny Bell sent for. I have to hurry home. Have a good evening—I mean, a good day."

"Yeah, the sun is freshly out."

"Yes, it is. Have a good morning, doctor."

Seeing that something was off with the sheriff, the doctor slightly smiled. "You as well, sheriff."

Sheriff Tuck had just learned that his wife had given birth. He turned to the storekeeper's wife. "I need something for a newborn."

"Has Jenny Bell given birth?"

"Yes, ma'am, she has."

"Well, I'll be. Boy or girl?"

The sheriff glanced over his shoulder at the doctor, then looked at the storekeeper's wife, whose grin had frozen on her face. "A girl. We have ourselves a baby girl."

"Well, I'm sure you don't need much. Jenny Bell and her grandmother came in a few months back and nearly shopped us out of everything a baby and a new mother could ever need. Umm..." She walked over to the toy section and picked out a multi-colored, mostly pink stuffed rabbit with long dangling ears. "Here, this should do."

The sheriff looked at the colorful stuffed animal, then back at the storekeeper's wife, who was still grinning. He smiled. "Yes, this will do just fine."

On his way home, he jumped off his horse, took the colorful stuffed animal from the horse's satchel, and tossed it in the woods just up the road from their cabin. Once he made it home, he tied up the horse and went to their bedroom.

Sheriff Tuck paused. He stopped in front of their bedroom door.

Jenny Bell sat in a rocker feeding the baby, waiting for the moment he would open the door for the first time after she'd given birth. "It's a girl, in case you're wondering."

"I wasn't." Turning away from her, he left their bedroom and went to the parlor. For the short time he was home, the sheriff was miserable, anxious to leave and return to his lover. Jenny Bell's tone had quickly turned him off. He started taking off his boots. "Is there anything to eat around here? Tondey!"

Tondey rushed to the parlor. "Yes, sir."

"I'm hungry. Get me something to eat."

"Yes, sir." Tondey walked away contemplating. "All I know how to cook are eggs and rice. I served it to the missus, she didn't complain. He'll get the same."

The sheriff sat on the settee with his elbows on his knees. With his hands holding up his face, he pouted like a child on punishment. "Going back into town so soon is not an option after the wife has just given birth. Surely, I could say my sheriff's duties call for my return, but that excuse would paint me as an uncaring husband and father. Not a good look for a future mayor. Just for the night. Just this night, then..." He lay back and stretched out on the settee.

Not long after, Tondey walked in with a bowl of burnt rice and eggs.

"He's asleep." He walked away mumbling, "Every time I try feeding y'all, y'all go to sleep."

The next morning, Jenny Bell awakened and found the sheriff standing over the crib of the cooing infant. She eased out of bed and stood next to her husband.

"I just wanted to have a look."

"She's perfect." Jenny Bell put her hand on his back and rubbed.

"She's a nigger, Jenny Bell."

"She's your child, husband. Your daughter."

He looked at her. "I would have liked that; I really would have, but your mother..." He turned to the baby. "...she took that away from me."

~~~~~

When Jenny Bell was just ten years old, all she knew of her mother was that she'd died while birthing her. That story became a problem when she walked to the door of the kitchen house and overheard Pearl, the cook, speaking to Peteney, the only other child on the plantation. She stayed hidden by the doorway.

"They killed 'im after she died. Like it was his fault that Jenny Bell's mama fell in love with 'im and died after she gave birth to his baby. You best leaves Jenny Bell alone before you end up like him."

"I's just playing wit' her, is all." The twelve-year-old boy was Jenny Bell's only friend.

"No more playing. We slaves work; we don't have time to play. Now, gone get to your ma and stay away from that child. Tell your ma Pearl said find you some chores to do before the overseer does."

Little Jenny Bell rushed off and hid on the side of the building just as the boy ran out of the kitchen house. She immediately took what she'd heard to her grandmother. "Pearl said they killed a slave 'cause my mother fell in love with him. And—and something about he was killed after my mother gave birth to his child. And she said for Peteney not to play with me anymore."

"Jenny Bell, you mustn't play with the slaves."

"But he's my friend. We're the only children who live here, grandmother. I have no one else to play with. He's a good slave. He does everything I tell him to do. He's no trouble."

"He's a slave, Jenny Bell. A nigger. You're a White girl and should never make friends with niggers. Mistakes can come from it. You have your dolls, lots of them to play with. Now, go on to your room. I'll send Izzy to get you off to bed. It's close to your bedtime."

"But, grandmother—"

"No buts. It's off to bed for you, little one."

"Yes, ma'am." Jenny Bell dropped her head and went to her room. Not feeling satisfied by the answer she'd received from her grandmother, as soon as Izzy left her room that evening, she jumped out of bed and snuck down the stairs, headed to her grandfather's office, and eased the door open.

"Jenny Bell, what are you doing out of bed? Isn't it your bedtime? Here, come kiss your grandpa goodnight and hurry off to bed."

She walked over to him and leaned against his leg. "Grandfather, I know my mother died while giving birth to me. But what about my father? What happened to him?"

He let out a deep sigh. "Your father, well, he was a man of honor. He fell from a horse and broke his neck. He never knew of you, but he would have been so proud of the young lady you're becoming."

"Was he a nigger?"

"What—why would you ask?"

"I heard Pearl say so in the kitchen house when she told Peteney not to play with me."

"I'm sure you heard wrong. Pearl would never tell a horrible untruth such as that."

She dropped her head. "I suppose so."

"Now, give me a kiss and get to your bed, young lady."

She kissed her grandfather and went off to bed.

Five years passed without a word of her father ever being mentioned. One day, at the age of fifteen, after leaving school, Jenny Bell marched up to the door of her grandfather's office and shoved it open. "Am I a nigger?" Jenny Bell's skin was like that of a tanned White girl. She had long, brunette hair, full lips, a perfect nose, and brilliantly shaped eyebrows.

Sitting behind his desk, her grandfather looked at the gentlemen politician who sat across from him. "If you would be so kind to allow me to speak with my granddaughter alone."

"Of course." Smoking a cigar, the older politician stood in his fine attire and left the room.

"Young lady, I would remind you to be respectful and thoughtful when entering my office where I often conduct business with important politicians. Knock and only enter after I invite you in. Now, to this outlandish business you speak of. Why would you let such lies come out of your mouth?"

"Everyone knows, grandfather. Everyone knows that my mother bedded a nigger. A *nigger* with green eyes and I carry his blood. My father wasn't a man of honor. He didn't break his neck after falling from a horse. He was a *nigger!* A black...smut...nigger, and I don't want to hear any more lies about his honor."

She stormed away and went directly to the kitchen house where she found Pearl standing in front of the wood-burning stove. "Pearl, you're the only one I can trust. Don't lie to me, please, Pearl, don't lie to me. Everyone lies to me about my mother and father. I need you to tell me the truth."

"What are you talking about, Ms. Jenny Bell?"

"I wanna know about my mother and father."

"About your ma and pa? It's...It ain't my place, child."

"But you know. You know more than I know." She stepped closer to Pearl. "All I'm asking for is the truth. The truth about my parents. I have a right to know."

Pearl wiped her hands on her apron and tended to the large pots on the stove. "Didn't your grandpa say, tell you about your ma and pa? It's for him to say, to tell you about your ma and pa."

"Please...please, I need to know why all the kids in school hate me. Everyone in school knows—everyone knows but me. Please, Pearl, tell me about my mother and father."

"I'on know what to tell you, child." Pearl was torn. She loved Jenny Bell and held a special place in her heart for her father and mother.

"You have to. No one else will. I deserve to know the truth and you know my grandparents will never grant me that."

"If I do, child, your grandpa, he'll have me killed. He'll have me strung up."

Jenny Bell stepped in front of Pearl. "I'll protect you. I promise. I won't let him hurt you. I won't tell him that I learned it from you."

Fear was all over Pearl's face. Deep thoughts clouded her mind, confusing her, leading her to speak the truth while knowing that she shouldn't. Pearl wiped her hands on her apron again. She walked over to a chair and sat. "They were fine folks, your ma and pa." She told her everything.

"Thank you. Thank you so much." Jenny Bell hugged Pearl and left the kitchen house. She went straight to her grandfather's office, turned the knob, and pushed the door open.

He immediately stood. "Jenny Bell. I thought I told you to never come into my office without kno—"

"Pearl told me everything, grandfather."

"She would never do such a thing. She would never tell you a lie—I told her, if she ever mentioned this again, I would have her hung."

"She confirmed everything the kids in school had already said." Jenny Bell saw when her grandfather's eyes went from straight to squinting with fury. "No more lies, grandfather. Is it true? Is it true that my father was a nigger?"

"...Yes...Where is Pearl?"

"Where she always is, in the kitchen house." Jenny turned and left her grandfather's office.

Pearl, the slave, who'd cooked for that family for thirty-two years. A large, dark woman with a round face, whom everyone loved, was stripped of her clothes in front of everyone, including her daughter and son-in-law. She was strapped to a tree and beaten. Then they tied a noose around her neck, sat her on a horse, and forced the horse to run. She was too heavy for the branch. It snapped and broke, dropping her to the ground.

"Finish her," Jenny Bell's grandfather ordered.

Taking his long knife from the side strap of his hip, the overseer went over to the mourning Pearl and split her neck from ear to ear. "'I'm gonna miss her good cooking." He cleaned the knife on his pants. "Best apple pies I ever had."

~~~~~

At the age of fifteen, Jenny Bell was a very beautiful young woman. Had her mother's secret died with her, she would no doubt have been an ideal pick of all suitors, but not with black blood in her veins. She was the stain of the White community in her town, and no young man ever looked her way. Their disdain for her caused her to hate herself.

"Don't worry, Jenny Bell," her grandmother would often encourage. "Your grandfather will find you a husband when the time comes."

Ten years passed and she'd turned twenty-five. She never went anywhere and sat alone in her room. She'd lost all hope of ever getting married until the sheriff, an old classmate who used to tease her about her "nigger father" came knocking. He'd left their town years ago and had returned to bury his father, the last of his parents. When Jenny Bell's grandfather learned that he was in town, he summoned him.

"What'dya think of my Jenny Bell?" Her grandfather asked the sheriff.

"What do you mean by that question?"

"She's quite the beauty, my Jenny Bell, don't you think?"

"Oh, I see. She is a very lovely woman, Victor, but surely you understand why I, nor any man, would have an interest in her."

"No, I wouldn't."

"She's a nigger, Victor. Everyone in town knows of her green-eyed pappy."

"That's what makes you the perfect mate for her."

"Me? How do you figure?"

"You live a couple of states over where no one knows of my Jenny Bell or...Well, there are no outward or any distinctive features or characteristics that show or tell of her mother's mistakes. Nothing but words, things that people around here don't even speak of anymore. Her mother's past is just that, the past. Jenny Bell shouldn't have to suffer for it. And of course, this favor doesn't come without benefits in return. What can I do for you?"

The sheriff sneered. "Well, since you asked...I do have a strong desire to become a major player in the political society." The sheriff shared his ambition of becoming the town's mayor, which would pave the way for his political future.

"I know the governor of your state personally. A governor who I happen to know plans to retire after a few more campaign seasons. I think you would make a fine replacement for him. Becoming mayor is the perfect place to start. I'm sure I can make that happen. Do we have a deal?" Victor stood with his hand stuck out for the sheriff to take.

The sheriff looked at his hand, then smiled. "You have a deal." He grabbed Victor's hand and shook it.

Chapter 42

On his second night home after the birth of their daughter, the sheriff awakened in the wee hours of the night. "This heat is sweltering." It was always much cooler in their bedroom with the two large windows opened. He made his way to their room and quietly slipped into their bed, trying not to disturb the sleeping Jenny Bell.

After being awakened by the baby and tending to her, she scooted up next to her husband in bed.

The moment he felt her, he got up, went back to the parlor, and sat. She followed, sitting next to him.

"Jenny Bell...that baby was born four months early. To my knowledge, babies don't survive when born that soon. And they're definitely not that size at birth. They're much smaller. That means you were already pregnant when I touched you. Either you tell me how, or I will walk out of that door and never return."

"I..." She told him of the night she'd gotten him drunk. "I'm sorry, husband, I wanted to make love to you for the first time...as your wife."

"No, you wanted to force a nigger child on me."

"No one here knows of the blood that runs through my veins but you and I. Why must you *always* bring it up?"

"Jenny, I ran into a childhood friend the other day. He asked how you were doing. He knows, and the moment he shares what he knows with someone in this town, I will never become mayor. Thanks to you and your nigger blood and now your nigger child, my political dreams will never come to fruition."

She reached out to touch him. "I'm sor—"

He pulled away. "I can't allow you to ruin my future." He turned to her. "The moment I win the mayor's seat, I will no longer need your grandfather's help."

"What does that mean?"

"I would suggest you think about it."

She stood and stared toward the stairway. "Sleep well, husband." She left the parlor.

~~~~~

Six months later, Tondey was holding the baby while Jenny Bell prepared breakfast for her husband. "You have the most beautiful eyes."

The baby started crying.

"Oh, not now. I must finish breakfast. Rock her, Tondey. Rocking soothes her."

He rocked the baby, but that didn't help. "Maybe it's time to feed her, ma'am."

"Gracious. She's going to awaken the sheriff."

"Here, take her and let me finish cooking." Tondey walked the baby to its mother.

"No, you'll burn it. And I need this to be perfect. Give her to me." He carefully placed little Delores into her mother's arms. She cooked, fed, and rocked the baby at the same time, and after the baby was full, Jenny Bell gave her back to Tondey. "Here, she needs burping and changing. While you do that, I'll take the sheriff his food."

She carried the platter to their bedroom where the sheriff was lying awake. "Husband...It's time to eat."

He sat on the side of their bed and took the plate from the platter.

"I do hope it's satisfying to your taste, husband."

He didn't say anything. Just stuffed the food down, held out the empty plate to her, stood, and started getting dressed.

"Where are you going? I was hoping that maybe we could spend the day together, as a family."

Taking his pants from the back of a chair, he slipped one leg into his trousers. "No time, Jenny Bell, I have a mayor's race to run, remember." He slipped the other leg in.

"Well, why don't you allow me to help?"

He threw on his shirt, picked up his suspenders, and started fastening them. "No, thank you. I have plenty of help."

"Husband, please, I'm your wife. It's my duty to assure your success. We can do this together. Please let me help. You spend so much time hating me for what I have no control over, that you overlook what I can offer you."

"What can you offer me? You offered enough when you gave me something I didn't want. You got me drunk and forced it upon me. There's nothing more you can offer me except to step aside and allow me to leave." He nearly pushed her out of the way.

"I often had the privilege of listening in on my grandfather's conversations. Although he never wanted a political role, he had the benefit of working with those who dreamed of becoming politicians. It was my grandfather who they came to—to manifest their dreams into reality."

The sheriff stopped getting dressed to listen.

"My grandfather was quite skillful and persuasive. And I sat at his feet throughout my years of growing up, learning everything there is to know about creating and running successful political campaigns. My grandfather spearheaded the campaign of every candidate who came to him, and each and every one of them won their bids.

"And you, my husband, have all his knowledge right before you. You would be foolish to not take advantage of it because of my past. Get your mind off the past, my dear husband, and think of your future and how I can contribute to it."

The sheriff slowly slipped his arm into one side of the suspenders then the other. While thinking, he grabbed his chin and slowly walked around the room. "I cannot so easily forget the past when our childhood friend is in town. If he says anything to anyone about your bloodline, I will be ruined."

"A dead man can't talk."

He looked up at her. No need to ask if she was serious, the look on her face showed it. "Are you suggesting—"

"My dear, husband, I would suggest you think about it."

Chapter 43

"Give her to me!" Taking the baby from Tondey, Jenny Bell lightly tossed the seven-month-old infant on the bed. "Find something to do. Go clean out the hog pen, the chicken coop, or chop some wood! All you do nowadays is fuss over Delores. She's mine, not yours. She has a father. She doesn't need a nigger fussing over her. Niggers have ruined our lives enough. First mine and the same thing will happen to her. Well, not if I can help it. She'll know to hate you all and why, I tell you. I'll teach her, I will. I'll teach her." Jenny Bell dropped to the floor, threw her head and arms on the bed, and cried.

"Ma'am, is there something I can do for you?"

Her head rested on her arm as she stared with a full mind and a heavy heart. She lifted her head and closed her eyes while the past burned her spirit. "I know you know of it."

"What, ma'am?"

"Living in this small house, I'm sure you've overheard it. My husband surely doesn't spare my feelings about bringing it up. I hate you, you know. I hate every one of you niggers."

"Ma'am, I ain't never did nothing for you to hate me for. I just do as I'm told when told to do it."

A look of evil was plastered on her face. "You were born Black, that's reason enough."

"That's a no-good reason."

"Why would you say that?"

"Say what?"

"What you just said."

"You mean, that's a no-good reason?"

"Yes, that. Where did you get that from?" Jenny Bell asked.

"I've always thought it, ma'am. And said it many times."

"It's what Pearl said his last words were."

"Who's last words?"

Jenny Bell got up from the floor and sat on the bed. She looked at Tondey, then the floor, and spoke of what she had been told. Her mind drifted back to that day when she was in the kitchen house, standing in front of Pearl. She opened her mouth and bled out the blood that ran through her veins.

"When I was fifteen, neither my grandfather, nor my grandmother would provide any answers, even after I'd learned the truth from school. I'd learned why the other kids would not play with me. I went to the only person who I knew could tell me and begged her to tell me about my mother and father. 'Pearl,' I said, 'you have to tell me the truth.' I remember her response as if it was today."

Jenny Bell stared at nothing and told Tondey about the conversation she'd had with Pearl."

~~~~~

Age 15

"If I do, child, your grandpa, he'll have me killed. He'll have me strung up."

Jenny Bell stepped in front of Pearl. "I'll protect you. I promise. I won't let him hurt you. I won't tell him that I learned it from you."

Fear was all over Pearl's face. She'll never know how sweet her pa was if I don't tell her. Although she shouldn't, Pearl looked directly into Jenny Bell's eyes. "For no-good reason."

"What? There has to be a reas—"

"No child, not always. It was his last words when your grandpa had 'im hung. 'You hates me for no-good reason,' he said. He had the saddest look in his eyes. Died with 'em opened. I'll never forget 'em. They were full of water.

"Your mama loved 'em, she did. She was so sweet. Not knowing nothing about hate, she fell in love with her childhood friend. It was me who caught 'em. I went through the barn on my way to the chicken coop to fetch eggs to make bread, and that's when I saw them. Him on top of her, clothes still on, but pulled down enough to see that more was going on. More than I wanted to know. They didn't see me, so I didn't say nothing. I rushed to the chicken coop and came out on the other side.

"Then your grandma learned that she was with child and took her out of school. But not before she told her best friend who told the other kids in school. That's how people knew. Your ma, she died while giving birth to you.

"Your pa, he was a good boy. He had the prettiest green eyes. First and only time I ever saw green eyes was on his face. By the time he was sixteen, he'd been on four plantations. This one was the last. I can tell you, he was a sweet child. He was raised by an old lady but when she died, the massa sold him off. On that plantation, the overseer raped him. Another slave beat the overseer when he learned of it.

"Then another massa sold him, he said, 'For no-good reason.' The place he was on before this one wasn't no plantation. Just a place where slaves worked hard to stay fit 'til they're sold to the next. That's how he ended up on this here plantation.

"He had a sad life, he did. Walt, that's his name. The name of your pa was Walt. Walt died, hung for loving your ma and making you."

~~~~~

Blinking her eyes, Jenny Bell returned from the spoken memory of learning that she had Black blood in her veins. "He should have died—he should have. He killed my mother by making her have me and then he ruined me. I hate him for it. He deserved everything that happened to him."

She kept a straight face while deep in thought. "I hated Pearl for telling me about him. She said it as if to be proud of that nigger's accomplishment. A slave who slept with a White woman, like she was proud of that. Proud of that nigger, Walt, for ruining my life with his blood. So, I told my grandfather where I'd gotten the information from."

Tondey's face wore shock. "You told him that Pearl told you? What happened to Pearl?"

With slightly raised lips, Jenny Bell smiled. "Pearl, the slave, who'd cooked for my family for thirty-two years. A large, dark woman with a round face, who everyone loved, was stripped of her clothes in front of everyone, including her daughter and son-in-law. She was strapped to a tree and beaten. Then they tied a noose around her neck, sat her on a horse, and forced the horse to run. She was too heavy for the branch. It snapped and broke, dropping her to the ground.

"'Finish her,' my grandfather said, as I stood by his side holding his hand. The overseer took out his long knife and sliced her neck from ear to ear."

"Why would you—"

"To erase all traces of that nigger's blood and the story she'd kept in her heart. The story she should have kept to herself. I'm going to make damn sure Delores never knows anything about him. *For no-good reason!* I have every reason to hate him."

Tondey's eyes and heart filled with anger. The thought of having Pearl killed. *And they killed my son. How many more times did the overseer rape him after I was sold? Then they hung him. Hung him because he was worth loving. And his daughter hates him because her ma loved him. My son was hung for being Black. Hating him because he was Black ain't no-good reason at all.* The very thought tore at his core. *Walt had White blood in him too, but that didn't matter. Any ounce of Black blood bears hate.* He was boiling with anger when the sheriff walked in.

"Tondey, leave us. I need to speak with my wife."

The baby started crying.

"Take Delores with you," Jenny Bell said.

"Yes, ma'am."

In the kitchen, Tondey could hear their outburst through the walls. He rocked little Delores. "You got the prettiest green eyes, just like my boy, your grandpa. One day, I'm gonna tell you all about him. Keep his story going like the brave Pearl did. Ain't I, old man? I see you sitting in that corner. What's about to happen now, huh?"

After their argument, in the pitch of the night, the sheriff left home.

Jenny Bell knew exactly where he was going "...To his mistress." Scorned, she got word to her grandfather the very next day, telling him of her husband's affair and explaining how he'd treated her and their daughter.

Victor, Jenny's grandfather, immediately came to their home and summoned the sheriff. "You be faithful to my granddaughter or else."

"Or else what, Victor?"

"I'll see to it that the mayor's seat is never yours. I'll see to it personally that your political future will never materialize."

"How dare you threaten me. I no longer need your help, Victor. The people in this town love me. I'll get their vote without you."

Victor, who'd always gotten his way, was enraged. "You obviously underestimate my power, sheriff." He stormed out of their home.

The sheriff sat back in his chair and downed a bottle of bourbon. "I don't need you to win. He took another long sip from the bottle.

Although the sheriff's childhood friend mysteriously disappeared, he still lost the mayor's race. Losing cost him everything. While running, he had left the sheriff's seat vacant and a new Sheriff won. With no job and no political prospect, he moved away with his lover, leaving Jenny Bell and the baby behind.

Chapter 44

Times were changing. Talk of the civil war was going on. Many slaves defected to the north to fight for their freedom. Others joined the Southern cause with promises of gaining their freedom should the south win the battle.

Jenny Bell never got a divorce but married a man who hated Blacks as much as she did. They raised little Delores to do the same.

With so much talk of ending slavery, Jenny Bell and her new husband grew even more bitter toward Blacks. Their lust of hate ran so deep, they took it out on the closest one to them, Tondey. His very dark skin emboldened their harsh treatment even more.

No longer allowed to sleep on the floor beneath the staircase once Jenny Bell remarried, Tondey slept on the porch like a beggar man and was only allowed to come in during the winter months or on rainy days. He'd gotten very ill, coughed a lot, and could hardly move due to pain and arthritis from previous beatings and the cold weather. Although the war had started, slaves were still not free. Sick, hurting, or cold, Tondey still had chores to fulfill and masters to obey.

"Get up." Looking down at Tondey, Jenny Bell nudged him with her foot. "Get up, nigger. I need wood for the stove. Go out and get what's chopped and bring it right back. Get it now." She walked away from him, toward the front door. "God, you stink."

Waking with pain, Tondey slowly got up while trying his best to hold onto the dirty blanket he slept beneath. He pulled on the strings used to keep the blanket tied around his neck and headed for the forest to collect wood as ordered. Once the chopped wood was collected, he carried the logs to the cabin, but tripped on a rock and fell, hitting his head.

Two hours later, long after Jenny Bell had expected him back, she thought aloud, "Where's that nigger?" She took off her apron. "Come on, Delores, let's go find that lazy nigger." They headed for the woods, not too far from their cabin, and found Tondey on the ground.

"Is he dead?" Delores walked up to him, drew back her leg, and kicked him in the head.

The blow awakened him. He coughed as if he was choking.

"Nope, he's still alive. Come on, Delores, your father will be home soon. Let's get dinner finished. I'll teach you how to make my Heavenly Pie, and you can teach it to your daughter, and she can teach it to her daughter. My famous apple pie recipe will be the family's pride and joy." She took her daughter's hand. "Tondey, get up. I need firewood for the stove this instant."

"Get up, nigger." Delores held her mother's hand.

"Yes..." He coughed. "Yes, ma'am."

Tondey crawled from the ground. When he got back to the house, he took the wood to the kitchen. Pain ached his entire body. Adding to it was a throbbing headache from Delores's kick. He started putting the wood in the oven.

"That's not enough wood. You should know that by now, Tondey. Niggers never learn."

"Ma'am, you said to bring what was chopped. That's it, that's what was chopped."

"No excuses. I need more wood."

"Yes, ma'am." He went back into the forest to chop more wood.

While preparing to cook the apple pie, Jenny Bell gave the last of the ingredients to Delores. "Go ahead, you may pour it in."

"*Like this*." Delores emptied the measuring cup.

"Yes, exactly like that."

Delores set the cup on the table and looked at her mother for further instructions.

"That's it. Everything I put in my apple pie is all in. Now, let's mix it." Jenny Bell began mixing. She gave a mixing wand to Delores. "Here, stir with me."

Together, they stirred the ingredients in the bowl. "There, all done."

"Can I go play now?"

Jenny Bell huffed and washed her hands on her apron. "I suppose so, since we're still waiting for more wood."

Little Delores went to the forest to find Tondey. Straying from the path, she spotted something in the woods. "What's that?" Slowly moving toward it, she reached for the item. It was a multi-colored, mostly pink stuffed rabbit, with long dangling ears covered in dirt. "How long have you been out here? You're so dirty." She threw the stuffed animal back into the woods and continued on her way to find Tondey. She came up behind him.

"What's that?" She pointed.

Picking up the wood he'd chopped, Tondey turned to see what she was referring to. "Oh, that, it's a but—" He coughed. "A butterfly." Turning his mouth away from her, he coughed again. "And it's green, just like your eyes."

"Did I get my eyes from green butterflies?"

"No, you got 'em from your grandpa."

"Who's my grandpa? Is he my mother's grandfather?"

Tondey laughed. "No, no." He coughed. "Your grandpa was a special person."

"Is that why his eyes were green? Because he was a special person?"

"No..." Tondey sat on a large log. Still holding the wood in his hand, he put them on the ground, looked at the trees and thought about Walt. *You never had a chance at life, my boy. This will be the only way I know how to help you live from beyond the grave.* He told her everything about her grandfather.

Little Delores raced back to the cabin as fast as she could. Running up the steps, she rushed straight to the kitchen where she found her mother. "Mommy, Mommy, he said my grandpa was a nigger."

"Who said so?"

"Tondey. He said that's where I get my green eyes. From my nigger grandpa." The six-year-old started crying and hugged her mother's hips. "I don't want a nigger for a grandpa."

Jenny Bell knelt and held her daughter by the arms. "There, there, Delores. Tondey's out of his mind. He's sick and doesn't know what he's saying."

"So, my grandpa isn't a nigger?"

"Look at your hands." Jenny Bell took Delores' hands and held them up. She pulled on her arms. "And your arms. Do you see how dark Tondey is?"

With tears drying on her face, Delores nodded her head.

"Does your skin look *anything* like his?"

She shook her head from side to side.

"Then what Tondey says isn't true. He's sick. He doesn't know what he's saying. He's stupid, too. All niggers are stupid. Are you stupid like niggers?"

Delores smiled. "No, *I'm not!*"

"Come here." She pulled her daughter in and hugged her.

Jenny Bell heard Tondey coughing before he came into the house. She looked at Delores. "Why don't you go to your room and play with the new doll your father bought you?"

"Yes, ma'am." Passing by Tondey, Delores skipped to her room. "My mommy said I'm not a nigger, nigger."

"And close the door, honey!" Jenny Bell listened for the door to close.

Tondey's cough got louder, telling her that he was near the kitchen. He went directly to the stove and started loading the logs into the burner.

"What did you say to Delores?"

Struggling to get up from his knees, Tondey dusted his hands together and turned to face her. He looked her directly in the eyes, knowing it was the first thing he'd learned not to do from Ms. Lora Dean's Plantation. "The truth, ma'am. I told her the truth."

Jenny Bell gave him a hard slap that shifted his face right.

He turned back to her. Staring into her eyes, he coughed directly in her face.

Rushing to cover her face, she became furious. She wanted to hit him again, but his boldness caused her to fear him.

He began walking away.

The very thought of him defying her enraged her. She released the fear. "Get back here, nigger. You get back here and take your punishment like a nigger."

"I have work in the garden to do, ma'am. You can find me there."

Tondey was on his knees working in the garden when Jenny Bell, her husband, and little Delores walked up behind him.

Jenny Bell's husband carried a shotgun. He pointed it to the back of Tondey's head and pulled the trigger.

Tondey fell over. Blood leaked from the hole in his head onto the ground and into the garden.

"Nigger!" He spat on Tondey's still body, and he, Jenny Bell, and Delores all went back in the house and ate the big meal she'd cooked.

"Time for dessert." Jenny Bell stood and took the lid off the pie doom.

"Yay! Apple pie. I helped Mommy make it! And I'm gonna teach my daughter how to make it, too."

Chapter 45

~~ 1990 ~~

"Your stomach's big, Millie. How many months are you?"

"Seven." Millie held her back and sat on the sofa in her aunt's trailer. "Yeah, um seven months, Aunt Carol, and you know what I've been thinking?"

"What's that?" Aunt Carol's southern accent was strong.

"Since um having a boy—did Mama tell you what I was thinking?"

"Yeah, I told her." Millie's mom, Christine, walked into her sister's trailer carrying a twenty-four-count case of beer. "Here's your case of Budweiser, Carol. I'll take 'em in the kitchen." An Alabamian at heart, Christine spoke like a country girl as well.

"Thank you. Put 'em on the kitchen table. I'll put 'em in the fridge later."

"So, back to what I was saying, Aunt Carol. Um having a boy and I wanted to give my son a family name."

Christine, a sizable woman, came back into the living room and collapsed into the sofa with a heavy whoosh. "Wooh. Yeah, we went through family names, but every name I gave her, she hates."

"What about Bill, our brother, who's your uncle? You know he ain't got no kids. That'll do 'im good to have a child in the family named after him." Carol looked at her sister. "Christine, would it worry you too much if I ask for one of them beers on ice?"

"On ice?"

"Yeah, you know I have to have it cold."

Christine struggled to get off the low couch. "You want anything else from the kitchen? It'll be my last trip in there."

"I'll have a smoke if you got one."

"That's why you're on that oxygen now, Carol. No cigarettes for you. I'll get you that beer on ice, though."

"Bring me two...And lots of ice...In a tall cup..." Carol turned back to Millie. "So, what do you think?"

"About what, you smoking?"

"No. 'Bout naming your son after your Uncle Bill. That'll sure make him proud. You know, with him being in prison and all."

"Aunt Carol, um not naming my son after no rapist."

"Well, I thought it was a great idea. Something to cheer him up. He's been awfully down in his letters to me."

"Here are your two beers and your tall cup with ice, Carol." Christine handed her sister a tall old white plastic cup with a hand-painted rebel flag on it. She sat back in the same spot on the couch she'd climbed up from earlier.

Millie continued. "No, I was thinking of an ancestor's name. Like a great, great, great-grandfather. You know, somebody from way back."

"On our family's side, right? Your dad ain't got nobody on his side worth being proud of."

"Don't you talk about my husband, Carol. I married a good man. His family might be God awful, but he's a good man."

"He ain't held a job since Millie was a baby, Christine. He's a bum and so is his family."

"He does odd jobs to help us get by."

"And you barely get by. Been that way for years."

Millie jumped in. "It will be from our side of the family. From you and Mama's side."

"Well, our daddy's name was—"

"Carol, I told her Pop's name, his brothers, and his dad's name. She asked around and learned that our great-granddaddy's name is Paul. Did you know his name was Paul?" Christine asked.

"I think I heard something about a Paul. You know Ma ain't tell us much."

"Well, Millie ain't like the name Paul, either."

"Then how far back do you wanna go, Millie? We don't know the names of everybody?" Carol took a drink of her beer.

"I want a name with a story behind it. Something my son can be proud of."

"Carol, can you think of anybody? I done told her every name I can remember." Christine attempted to cross her legs, but her thighs and stomach prevented her.

Squeezing her lips together, the thin little Carol, whose size was the opposite of her sister, dropped her head and thought. "Christine, you remember that summer we visited grandma after she'd moved her ma, our great-grandma, in with her?"

"Yeah." Christine turned to her daughter, Millie. "Our great-grand-mama was senile. Always bringing up things from the past that no one could make sense of."

Carol took over. "She'd pull all sorts of stuff out of the air. But I remember her mentioning this one name. Used to say it all the time. You remember, Christine?"

"Yeah, what was it?"

"Walt."

"Yeah, that was it. Walt." Christine sat at the edge of the sofa.

"You had to put the pieces of the puzzle together. But I think she was trying to say he was her great, great, great grandpa if I'm counting right. Is that right, Christine?"

"I think so."

"But you do remember her talking about him?" Carol asked.

"Yeah, she said something about a Walt...about him killing a nigger. Blew his head off for talking back to his wife." Millie's mother leaned over to her. "This was when our family owned slaves."

Millie looked surprised. "We owned slaves?"

"Yeah, our family was slave owners. Ain't that right, Carol?"

"Yeah, I heard we owned lots of 'em. Had a big plantation and a big house too. Don't know how we lost it all and ended up living in a trailer park." Carol looked around her house.

"I like that story and that name. Walt. That's what I'm gonna name my son. Walt Mason, a nigger banging badass."

Chapter 46

The principal sat across from Mrs. Millie Mason and spoke to her about Walt, her son.

"Mrs. Mason, Walt and his friends continue to pick on the only African American child in their classroom, and I cannot allow that type of behavior in my school. I really need you and your husband to speak with him. Help him understand how offensive the "N" word is." Looking at Millie Mason, he knew his words were landing on hollow ground. "Due to the nature of his blatant disrespect of others and using the "N" word, he is being suspended for ten days. If it happens again, he will be dispelled for the rest of the school year."

Millie stood. "C'mon, Walt. I guess you'll be homeschooled from now on."

"I'm sorry to hear that. I would have hoped that this would be a teachable moment about racism."

"Are you calling me a racist, Principal Monroe? I don't coward to no one. Least of all, a Black principal in a predominately White county and school system. Remember your place. You're in my neck of the woods, and I know where you live."

"Are you threatening me, Mrs. Mason?"

Mrs. Millie Mason smiled. "You have a good day, Mi-ster Munroe. C'mon, Walt. Tell your ex-school principal goodbye."

"Bye, nigger."

"Well done, son. That earns you a slice of apple pie."

The Mason's household never shied away from their relationship with White supremacy and other racist groups. Their rebel flag hung proudly on a very tall pole for neighbors to see near and far.

On the third day of Walt's suspension, a social worker knocked on the door of their outdated single-wide trailer. She looked around at the overgrown grass. *I pray to God I don't step on a snake when going back to my car.* She stood mindfully on the top tier of the four thin steps, afraid that if she moved the wrong way, she would fall.

The door opened.

The social worker jumped, almost falling back. She quickly grabbed the door frame and found her balance. She smiled. "Hi, I'm Mrs. Tonya Fitzgerald with school social services." Mrs. Fitzgerald was a small woman with a big gut that made her look pregnant.

"I ain't asked for no social service's visit. What, you're trying to take my boy from us for using the "N" word or something?"

"That's not the reason for my visit. I assume that you're Mrs. Millie Mason."

"Yeah, that's me. What do you want?" Millie looked the short White woman over. "Hold on." She slammed the door and made the woman wait several minutes before returning. "Come in."

During their conversation, the school social worker was able to convince Mrs. Mason to allow Walt to return to school, "—where he can get a well-structured education in a constructive social environment. You are welcome to your views, Mrs. Mason. No one is trying to force you all to change them, but we do live in a society where we must be a part of those of all races and backgrounds. And

Walt will have to learn how to live in this society, whether you want him to or not."

"Mmhm." Mrs. Mason hated to admit it, but she knew the social worker was right. "I'll think about it. Lemme talk to his father. See what he says."

The social worker stood to leave. "What's that heavenly smell?"

Mrs. Mason smiled proudly. "It's my apple pie. An old family recipe. Would you like a piece? It's cooling."

The social worker looked down at her huge gut that had persisted past the births of her three children. "I would love to, but I shouldn't. As you can see, I need to keep away from calories." She left.

Walt returned to school after his suspension.

In his fourth-grade science class, the teacher Mrs. Duncan, called him to her desk. "Walt, while you were out, the class was assigned to a project where they paired up into groups. One team has one member too many. With your return, one of those students will become your partner." She turned to the classroom. "Leon, please come here."

Leon, a very dark-skinned kid, walked up to the teacher's desk.

The teacher put her hand on Leon's back. "Walt, you and Leon will be partners for this project. Now Walt, we won't have any problems, will we?"

Looking down, Walt shook his head. "No."

For their project, they had to catch a green anole lizard, research its origin, and teach what they learned to the class. At first, Walt showed no interest in the project or working with Leon. But Leon was funny. Wanting to be a comedian, he always told jokes that made Walt laugh, which made him excited for his fourth-period class to start.

"I got something for you," Walt said to Leon while they were outside in search of the green anole lizard one day. Walt pulled a brown bag from his book bag.

"What's that?"

"My mama's famous apple pie."

"Famous? She sells it in the stores?"

"No, but she should."

"Lemme see. I'll be the judge of that." Taking the pie, Leon bit into the slice.

Walt watched Leon's facial expression turn to pure enjoyment.

"Man, that's good."

Walt smiled. "I told you." He took out a piece for himself. The two finished the slices of pie and returned to their project.

Walt really enjoyed the task and working with Leon, who was quick and could jump high. "You're gonna be a basketball player. All niggers, I mean, all Blacks can play sports."

"Why did you say the "N" word?"

"Um sorry. I didn't mean to. I tried to fix it."

Leon gave him an offensive stare, then giggled. "Um, just kidding, man. It's okay. We're friends. I won't hold it against you if you never use it again."

"I won't." Walt looked past him and pointed. "Oh, look, there's one."

The two slowly crept up behind the fast green anole lizard and waited for the perfect time to... "Got it!" Walt quickly snared it. They took a closer gaze at the perfect creature.

"Wow." Leon looked into Walt's eyes. "It's almost the same color as your eyes. I've never seen green eyes before. No one can call you the blue-eyed devil. I mean, well, you know what I mean."

"No, I don't. Why did you call me a devil?"

"No, I said no one *can call* you a blue-eyed devil. That means you're not one. You understand?"

"I guess so."

Leon patted Walt on the back. "C'mon, let's go show Mrs. Duncan."

In that class, Walt was best friends with Leon. When he was in his other classes, at home, or out playing with friends, he fought with his conscience about hating Black people and made sure to keep his friendship with one a secret, but it wasn't long before his best friend Roy confronted him.

"Walt, Andrew said he saw you playing with that nigger in your science class."

"We have a class assignment together. I pretend he's my friend to get him to do all the work. Stupid, nigger."

They both laughed.

"You know me, Roy. I hate anyone who's not White."

"Yeah, me too," Roy agreed.

Proving it to everyone forced Walt to prove it to himself.

After that school year ended, Leon's family moved away, removing the two-sided guilt Walt struggled with while being torn between racism and having a Black friend. With Leon gone, he easily reverted to his old self. Absorbing the persuasion of the racist world that surrounded him. He learned to hate African Americans, Jews,

Indigenous Americans, and those of Asian descent for "no-good reason."

Walt never finished high school but landed a job at a chicken plant where he later became a line leader. He married a hometown girl and the two tried for years to have a child with no luck.

"It's me." Walt took the blame. "I can't give you a baby, Claire," he said to his wife.

"What if we go to one of those places to help get us pregnant?"

"A doctor won't change things. I ain't never been able to make a baby, no matter who I've been with."

One day, while driving through town in his 1980 F-150 Ford pickup truck with his childhood friend, Walt tried to run over a pedestrian who was just about to cross the street. Later that evening after leaving a meeting, he tried a second attempt at hitting the same old Black man, and again, he failed. Instead, his truck hit the side of a bridge, shot into the air, and landed upside down near a river, leaving his body distorted and broken.

Chapter 47

"Hello?" The man on the phone was barely awake.

"John Jr., it's four a.m. and Walt ain't home yet. Y'all still at the meeting?"

"Claire?"

"Yes, it's me. Walt never came home. I tried calling 'im, but he ain't answering. Are you with 'im?"

"Naw, Claire. Walt left the barn before I did. Said something about an apple pie."

"His mama dropped off a pie yesterday. You have any idea where he might be?"

"Naw, he said he was going home right after the meet. That was around...one this morning. He ain't there?"

"No, he never came home. I've been up all night waiting for him, and he ain't showed up. John, Jr., I have to ask you..."

"Claire, Walt ain't out with some other woman. That man loves you. If he ain't come home, that means something happened." John Jr. turned toward the floor where he planted his feet. "There ain't but thirty minutes from the barn to your house. You call the police, and I'll get some guys to go out with me to look for him. Trace his tracks."

"Thanks, John Jr. Um sure he's all right, right?"

"Yeah, yeah. We're gonna find him, Claire. Don't you worry. And if some nigger done harmed him, we gonna take care of that too."

~~~~~

In search of Walt, John Jr.'s truck pulled up on the Old Wood River Bridge. He and Roy jumped out and immediately started looking around.

"If he's not here, he probably drove into one of those fields." John Jr. walked toward the wall of the bridge. "Hey, looks like somebody done hit this wall." He looked around and spotted Walt's truck in the dark. It was upside down near the river. "Roy, I see his truck!"

They ran to the vehicle and found it badly damaged. Their attempts to open the doors failed.

Roy got on his knees on the moist ground near the river and looked inside. "I see 'im."

John Jr. rushed to the other side of the truck.

"Walt! Walt! Walt, you hear me?" Roy continued calling.

"Is he alive, Roy?" John Jr was slow to kneel.

"I'on know, John Jr. He ain't moving, he ain't—"

Walt coughed.

"Walt! Hey, man, you all right?" John Jr. was finally on the ground and looking in the truck.

"Naw, he ain't all right. Look at 'im. He's bent all out of shape. Walt, you hear me, friend? It's Roy. Don't worry, we gonna get you out of there." Standing on his knees, Roy pulled his phone from his pocket, and called 911.

"What you want now, old man? Every time you come, somethin—" Walt passed out.

"Walt! Walt! Stay with me, man. Hang in there." John Jr. yelled.

Roy's phone was pressed to his ear. "Hurry up. Get an emergency truck out here right now! We're on the Old Wood River Bridge...Yeah, that's my number. Get somebody out here right this minute... He's unconscious, and we can't get to 'im. He's trapped in his truck that's upside down... No, he ain't talking, he's unconscious... Okay... Yeah, right away... I will... Okay." Roy hung up.

John Jr. stood. "We're gonna lead the authority right out here, and we ain't that far from the barn. We wanna do that? They're gonna ask us why he was out here and how we knew to look here. That ol' nigger loving Sheriff's gonna interrogate us into bad health."

"Our sheriff is a White man married to a Black gal. What's wrong with men like that? We need to kill him right out here—tonight."

John Jr.'s phone rang. Removing it from its side holster, he looked at it. "It's Claire... Hey... Yeah, we found 'im... He's all right, just a little accident with the truck but nothing to worry about... Naw, don't worr... Claire, we done already called. The emergency truck's on the way... Naw, he's fine. Ain't no reason to worry. I'd tell you if he wasn't... No, he can't come to the phone right now. He was hurt some, and it's hard for 'im to talk... No, I said I would tell you if he was... Yeah, it's on the way... Yeah, yeah, you can meet us at the hospital... I will. I'll let you know anything changes. Alri... Yeah... Oh-okay... Ah-alright... We will." Putting his phone back in the holster, John Jr. got back on his knees. "She's worried and has a reason to be."

"You reckon we need to try and pull him out?" Roy looked in the truck to see if there was anything they could do.

"Naw, might make it worse. Might break something." He looked into the truck. "Walt! Walt! The emergency truck's on the way. Walt, stay with us, man. I need you to stay right here with us. John Jr. and Roy are right here for you."

Chapter 48

~~ Awakening ~~

Broken in several places, suffering from a head injury, and bleeding from within, Walt had two surgeries, four weeks of touch and go, and spent most of that time in a coma.

His wife, Claire, remained by his side as often as the hospital staff would allow her. She'd learned that the longer he was in a coma, the less possibility of recovery he had. So, with hands clasped across his belly, a dropped head, and closed eyes, she prayed. "God, please bring my hus—did he move?" She looked at him and hung on to hope while observing his still body. *Nothing.* Once again, she dropped her head and resumed prayer.

Another jerk from his body gave her the evidence she'd hoped for. She stood. "Walt?" Putting her hand to his forehead, she rubbed it. "Walt, it's Claire. Baby, open your eyes for me."

An oxygen mask covered his mouth and nose.

She watched while he struggled to open his eyes. Claire cupped one of his hands. "Walt, c'mon, baby, open your eyes." She kept rubbing his forehead.

Walt's eyes slowly opened and stared deathly toward the ceiling. He blinked several times.

Overjoyed, Claire started to cover her smile but grabbed and kissed his hand. "You stay right here, baby. I'll be right back." She left his bedside and ran down the hallway. "Nurse! Nurse!" Stopping in front of the nursing station, she leaned over the counter. "Where's my husband's nurse?"

"Who is your husband, dear?"

"Walt Mason, he's awake. He was in a coma, but now he's a—"

"Awake. Got it." The nurse looked up. "I'll send his nurse right in." She smiled.

"When?"

"As soon as—there she is."

Claire turned to see the nurse walking up behind her. "My husband, he's awake. Can you come and check on him?" Claire's emotions spilled through her eyes that leaked with joy.

"Absolutely." The nurse patted her back.

When they entered the room, Walt was looking around, giving in to the proof of what his eyes were providing. That he was waking up in a hospital room full of hospital equipment and not some old shack.

"Mr. Mason, how are you feeling?" The nurse walked up to the monitors and immediately started doing things to them.

He tried to talk, but his words came out croakily.

"Don't worry, speaking will come later."

With hands clasped on her chest, Claire watched nervously as she restrained the excitement of celebrating her husband's awakening.

The nurse asked Walt several more questions. Most he couldn't answer because his voice wouldn't release the words that came to his mind. Other questions she asked him, he had no thoughts about them. Walt looked bewildered, confused, sad even, like he'd been in a coma for years.

The nurse turned to leave the room, but Claire stepped in front of her. "How's he doing?"

The nurse smiled. "I think he's going to be all right. His vitals are a little elevated. Orientation is a little off, but those things are to be expected after an awakening. I have to report his consciousness to the doctor." She smiled again and left the room.

Claire went to Walt's bedside and gave him a humble smile.

He went for the oxygen mask to try and speak.

"Don't. You have time. Just rest." Her southern dialect was uncanny. She rubbed his arm that lay on his side. "Boy, I really missed those pretty green eyes."

"Pa—"

"Shhh...hush, now. The nurse's checking with the doctor."

In walked the doctor with the nurse behind him. "Mr. Mason, welcome back. How are you feeling?"

Again, he tried to speak, but he was hoarse and barely audible.

The doctor performed several physical examinations to Walt's arms and legs, while asking him to respond. "Mr. Mason, I'm going to have some blood drawn and order some brain images. We'll take it from there. I'll return after we get the results of those tests..." He looked at Mrs. Mason. "...and answer any questions you all may have at that time. Okay?"

Claire nodded and smiled.

The doctor and nurse left.

Walt pulled the oxygen mask from his face.

Claire rushed to stop him. "Let's keep that on." She put it back on.

"Paty."

"Who's Paty?"

Chapter 49

"Where is he?"

"He's right here." Claire looked toward the entryway to see John Jr. walking in.

He'd brought with him a huge grin. "There he is. Boy, you're awake. I ain't doubt for a minute that you'd come back to us. Look at you, looking all good. You see this woman here?" John Jr. threw his arm around Claire's shoulder and shook her. "She's been here praying for you every day. Walt, you got yourself a mighty good woman in this lady."

Although the oxygen mask was no longer on his face, Walt was still having difficulty with words. "John Jr.?"

"Yeah, it's me in the flesh. How're you feeling?"

"I be...Um..."

"Man, you're alive and woke. That's all that matters. You're awake. After you have some of that therapy, you'll be back to your old self in no time."

Claire's phone rang. Answering it, she signaled with a finger that she was going outside to talk.

John Jr. waited for her to leave. "Man, we're so glad to have you back."

Now in a regular hospital room, Walt turned away from John Jr. and planted his attention on the wall in front of him, trying to mentally put everything into perspective. The voices, the personalities, the room...his sanity.

The CT scan and physical examinations had showed that with therapy, he should be fine. However, the doctor could not say how long it would take or whether he would recover with the full capacity of all his physical functions and with all his memories intact since he was still having trouble speaking, understanding where he was, who he was, and what year it was.

As Tondey, he had awakened several times and in different places. Now he was being referred to as Walt. He found it hard to believe and even more challenging to adjust to about where he was and how to break free from where he had been. "This is a hospital, right?"

"Sure is, and man, you're back with us. Back from that coma that had you gone for a while."

"Coma?"

"Yeah, man. Nearly five weeks. Now it's time to get back to life, back to living. How long will it be before you can go home? The doctor say yet?"

A questionable look came across Walt's face.

Claire walked in. "Are you having a good visit with John Jr., baby?"

"He ain't saying much. He has to get back to his ol' self."

Claire rubbed Walt's arm. "He's getting there. One day at a time, ain't that right, baby?"

Walt didn't respond.

"Yeah, that's my boy. I know he'll snap back in no time. Welp, I have to get out of here and get to my place. Walt, we need you back at work. You can't be there from this bed."

"I'll take good care of him, John Jr. We have to get you back to work, don't we, baby?"

"Hey, hey, hey." Millie, Walt's mother, entered the ICU room carrying a covered dish. "John Jr. is that you?"

"It's me in the flesh. What'dya got there, Mrs. Millie?"

She lifted the towel that was spread over the dish. "His favorite dessert, apple pie. You wanna slice?"

John Jr. slapped his stomach. "Naw, I'll let Walt enjoy his pie. Mrs. Millie, if that pie of yours don't bring him back, I don't know what will."

"That's what um hoping."

"Lemme get out of here. Walt, my boy, I'll see you tomorrow. Claire, let me know if anything changes. Bye, Mrs. Millie." He left.

Carrying the dish, Millie walked to the foot of Walt's bed. "Walt, honey, how're you feeling?"

He didn't answer, just stared at her.

She looked across Walt's bed at Claire. "How's he doing, Claire?"

"He's slowly coming back to us...but he'll get there."

"Your dad's at work. Said he'll visit later. Look at what Mama brought you. A little help to rush the healing process." She got closer to Walt's bed. "Walt? Walt, honey. Look what Mama brought you." She pulled the towel off the dish. Passing it to Claire, she removed the lid from the dish and put it to Walt's nose. "You smell that?

That's the family's famous recipe. Your favorite, apple pie. Just pulled out the oven."

Walt looked up at her. "Apple pie?"

She smiled. "Yes, son, your favorite."

"Ma?"

"Yes, son?" Tears welled in her eyes.

"Where did that pie come from?"

"He's talking." Claire became excited.

"I knew this pie would do the trick. I cooked it, son. Just for you, I cooked it."

"No. The um...ah..."

They could see the frustration on his face as he struggled to make out what he wanted to say.

"Walt, don't worry yourself." Claire took his hand.

"Rea-ci...pee. Where did that...re-cee-pee come from?"

"You know, Walt. It's passed down through the family."

His squinting eyes showed how hard it was to force out his words. "F-f-from who?"

She looked at Claire, then Walt. "One of my great-great-great Grandmas. One 'em from way, way back?"

"H-how'd you know?"

"'Cause it's what my ma told me and what her ma told her. Why, Walt? What are these questions for?"

Claire spoke up for him, "Ma, you have to remember, he's still trying to remember things."

"It ain't no f-f-fam...mee-lee re-ci-pe."

Tension rested on Millie's face. "What're you saying, Walt? You can't talk, but when you do, you say this pie ain't no family recipe?"

"Ma, he's confused. He doesn't know—"

"Claire, I can hear with my own ears. He's saying this pie ain't no family recipe. He's calling me and my ma liars?" Millie always had a quick temper and easily jumped to whatever conclusion was formed in her mind.

"He's not saying that, Ma. He's not himself right now."

Walt continued squeezing his eyes tightly and struggled with every word. "I know...what um saying...What um asking. Did my family...come up...with-with, the re-cee-pee for that pie? Ma, you don't really know—do you?"

"Walt, where's this coming from?" She looked at Claire. "Where's this coming from?"

"I told you he's not himself, Ma."

"Claire, um—um...um awake now. Nnno coma. I don't... I don't...need you speaking f-f'me." He looked at his mother. "Ma, I...I—have...h-hard truth for you."

She stared into his eyes as if he'd already revealed that shocking truth.

Chapter 50

Walt was moved to a rehabilitation center for physical, speech, and occupational therapy. He was talking better and recalling his thoughts faster. Lying in the bed with closed eyes, his eyes swung open when hearing a man's voice.

"Walt! Walt, my man." Roy came in gleaming with excitement. He was loud, rowdy, and loved for his cheerful personality. "Well, look at you sitting there. You're looking mighty fine to these old, tired eyes. Gimme that hand, man, lemme shake it."

Taking Walt's hand, Roy slapped the back of it and shook it. When he released it, Walt looked at his hand from front to back. He missed seeing the dark skin that branded his race.

"I see you staring at that hand. Yeah, you're back. This here is the real world. Man, we thought you were a goner for sure. When me and John Jr. found you, we both thought that was the end of you. All I could think about was how I was gonna tell Claire. But you did it, man, you survived that crash and came back from the dead. You one tough rooster-ass son of a gun.

"Glad to have you back, Walt. I've been trying to get in and see you for a while, but man, we're short at the mill. Lazy ass monkey niggers don't wanna come to work. You give 'em a job, they complain about the pay. You give 'em the pay, they complain about the hours."

"That's because the Whites got it better."

"What do you mean?"

"They've always been paid more. They don't have reasons to complain. They have the pay and more vacation and sick days than Blacks. So, when they take off, they get paid. Shoot, I became a boss, but not because I could do the job better. There are others who've been there longer than me, work harder, and people I know who can do the job better, but I got promoted. Get paid more, have more time-off days, and stand around, for the most part, doing nothing. Talking to you and John Jr. most of the time. Since they get paid less, they can't even afford to pay for the insurance the company offers. It ain't right, Roy."

Roy dug his hands in his pocket. "White man privilege, Walt, what can I say? We're the superior race, man. You got your rightful place in the company. Don't spend no time arguing over monkey's rights. They got their rightful place in the company, too. We gave 'em jobs, didn't we? I think that coma done mixed up your emotions or something. Got damn monkeys. Who gives a rat's ass about 'em?"

Walt shook his head.

"Walt, that ain't your fight, man. You, me, we have other things to worry about. Like our monthly meetings that we ain't had since your crash. We stopped everything to try and keep that nigger loving sheriff off our asses. With your accident happening so close to the barn, the leader thought it best to hold off for a while. He ain't want the authorities seeing too many vehicles headed and coming from that way. Especially so late in the night. He said you can't be too careful."

"The barn. The meet. Yeah, I remember."

"Yeah, yeah! I knew you would come around. Just needed some memories to help you out. And our annual ritual, man that's been put off too. You know it was supposed to be next month. The leader said it's best to wait for that, too. If I had my way, I'd put a noose around a monkey's neck tonight. You know I've had it ready for a while. I'm gonna personally slip it over a nigger's head. Ritual or not. That's why I need you out of this bed and out hunting with me."

"What ritual?"

"I reckon that coma done darn near wiped your memories clean. Don't worry, my friend, I'll help you get it back. He looked at the door and leaned toward Walt. "The ritual is when we hang us a nigger."

Something inside Walt balled up. He thought about the story of them trying to hang Pearl and the branch that broke from her weight. He closed his eyes and visited memories of the whip coming across his back. Strikes that he never remembered stopping because each time he was beaten until he passed out. *And my boy.* "He raped 'im." Tears swelled in his eyes. "My innocent boy. He beat and raped him," he mumbled. An angry look came on his face.

"What's that, Walt?"

Walt looked at Roy. He was too overcome with anger and sadness to respond. Instead, he placed his eyes on a wall and recalled when he was in the fourth grade and had befriended Leon, a tall, skinny Black kid. Like someone who'd lived their life in the closet, Walt's love for his friend never came out. He'd buried that friendship deep within himself, from himself. From that part of himself who knew racism was wrong. "Even at the age of nine, I knew hating someone for the color of their skin was wrong."

"Walt, what're you saying, man?"

Living the life of Tondey, a dark man, Walt had received the same ignorant hatred he'd bestowed on others. He looked around his room and stopped on his feet with a motionless face. "Why do you hate 'em, Roy?"

"What?"

He turned to Roy. "Why do you hate 'em?"

"Who, Blacks? Jews, Asians, Mexicans, Arabs, In'yins, and all those other mixed breeds?"

"Yeah."

"'Cause they ain't us. Niggers ain't nothing but a bunch of low-class lazy asses with a lotta children that we have to take care of because they're on welfare. We give 'em free money, and what do they do with it? Buy watermelon and chicken.

"I saw one of 'em in the store the other day. Some Aunt Yo'mama bitch ordering five pounds of crabs with food stamps, so she can take 'em home to feed her lazy ass jobless ol' man. They're using my hard-earned tax dollars to buy expensive seafood. If they don't wanna earn money by working, they might as well be slaves."

Walt stared at him. "So, you hate a woman because she bought crabs with food stamps? How do you even know she paid for them with food stamps?"

"'Cause she used a card. Steaming hot crabs too. Smelling good."

"She paid with a debit card or a food stamp card?"

"'I'm sure it was a food stamp card."

"You saw it?"

"I didn't have to."

"You can't buy hot food with food stamps, Roy. I know. My great Aunt Carol done tried plenty of time. Hell, my ma too."

"So. It doesn't matter what you can buy with food st... Hey, man, hold your horses. What's gotten into you, man? That coma done mess your head up or something? This ain't you talking. Everything um saying, you done said. We saw it. We've been seeing 'em all our lives. Since we been growing up, we've been seeing Black folks living off the government."

"And White folks don't?"

"That's 'cause they need the help."

Walt looked at his hands again. He turned to the corner of the room, hoping to see the old man staring back, but the corner was empty. He'd long realized that he not only missed seeing the old man, but longed for his quiet company. "For no-good reason."

"What? What did you say?"

His slavery dialect had transitioned back to his southern accent, but his memory of the life he'd lived as Tondey was still fresh. "You know, Roy, I wasn't born racist. It was taught to me. Like you, I hated Blacks for no-good reason. Everything you just said, none of it was a good got-damn reason to hate somebody. 'Cause they bought crabs. What kind've shh...Man, just think about it. Black folks can't even buy crabs without being judged."

Roy chuckled. "Walt, it's me, man. What happened to you while you were in that coma? Just a few weeks back, you tried to run over one of 'em. You go in a coma, wake up, and you come out like this. Like I...*that we* hate Black folks for no-good reason, when I've named you every good reason to hate 'em."

"What, 'cause some of them are on welfare, you hate 'em? 'Cause they eat chicken and watermelon, you hate 'em. Buy crabs."

"This is one of those coma side effects, that's what this is. The Walt I know ain't this man sitting in front of me talking hog crack. You've been back a little over a month? You're still not yourself."

Roy rubbed his short red beard. He took off his hat, scratched his head, and put it back on. "C'mon, Walt, man, shake this off. We need you back. We need you with us for...." He looked at the door and whispered. "...for our next ritual. C'mon, man, we got some killing to do. You said this year was gonna be the year you take one out, remember? Instead of us spending time planning, you're sitting here taking up for these niggers...a bunch of lying thieves who rape and kill people."

Walt chuckled. "Yet, my ancestors stole a Black woman's recipe and called it theirs. Hell, White folks stole a whole damn country from them In'yins you hate. We stole a whole race of people, slaved, killed, and raped them."

"What can I say, man? We're the dominant race. It had to be done. White folks don't talk about what they want, they go out and get it. We don't beg for it like a bunch of lazy asses; we take it!"

Walt dropped his head to hide the tears that were growing. *God, I used to think like that.* "I heard about this story. A kid. Couldn't have been no more than ten. A curly hair kid with the most innocent smile. He loved playing." Walt smiled. "And making you laugh. He was just...sweet. But he was born in the eighteen hundreds, so that made him a—"

"Slave."

Walt looked at Roy. "Yeah...that's right. He was a slave. The kid didn't have a ma because he'd been sold from her. Every day he'd take bread and water to the field for the slaves. The overseer would take his whip and...and hit 'im. Over and over again. For no-good reason, he would smack that kid with his whip, make 'im drop the water and bread, then beat 'im with that same whip for dropping them. He even made him suck up the water from the dirt and eat the bread that was full of it. At night, he'd get that same boy, take 'im somewhere and rape 'im." Walt looked at Roy. "So, who's wrong in that story, Roy? The innocent slave boy being raped or the rapist?"

"What do you want me to say, Walt? I mean, slaves were possessions. We could do whatever we wanted to 'em."

"Get the hell out of my room, Roy."

"What?"

"You heard me. If you don't have compassion enough for an innocent child being raped by a nasty, mean White man, well...there's no hope for you."

"Walt, I guess you're a nigger lover now."

"Some people change, Roy, and sadly, some don't. Yeah, um a nigger lover. Proudly. Now, get the hell out of my room."

Chapter 51

Claire walked into Walt's room at the rehabilitation facility wearing animal patterned scrubs. She worked as a childcare giver at a daycare center. A simple-looking, average-height girl, Claire's dark permed hair rested on her shoulders. Although she didn't have any children of her own, she loved working with them. Her job and Walt were her replacement for children.

Claire adored her husband. Being home without him and thinking that she would lose him left her depressed. To have him back, brought out the cherry color in her pale cheeks, and her smile showed it. Walking into Walt's room, she found two ladies who had only recently entered. They turned to her.

"Hey, baby. What's going on here?"

The White woman of the two responded. "Hi, I'm Linda, Mr. Mason's physical therapist. And this is Dyesha, she'll be taking over for me next week." She stuck out her hand to greet Claire, who shook it.

Dyesha was a small, tanned-skinned woman in her late twenties. She wore long extended braids adorned with a few pieces of African-style wooden beads. She stretched out her hand to greet Walt. "Mr. Mason, I'm glad to be working with you."

Walt took Dyesha's hand and looked directly into her eyes.

Claire noticed.

Releasing his hand, Dyesha put both her hands in her pocket and took a step back.

"Ain't nobody else here who can give him therapy?" Claire removed her purse from her shoulder and set it on the chair.

Linda looked at Claire. "You mean like another physical therapist?"

"Yeah. Someone who looks more like me." She removed her jacket and also placed it in the chair.

"I hope I'm getting this wrong. Of course, you don't mean someone White?" Linda looked at Claire for a response.

"If we have a preference, yes, that's what I mean."

"Mrs. Mason, you have no say over who treats your husband in this facility. We have only one PT here, and that person is Dyesha. She's well versed in her field. If anyone can get your husband up and walking again, she can. That should be your only concern. Not the color of her skin. What are you, some sort of racist?"

"'Unless she's changing his piss pan, we don't need a—"

"Claire, you're out of line."

They all turned to Walt.

"Ms. Dyesha, I'll gladly take your services and apologize for my wife. She can be overbearing at times."

Moving from Pennsylvania to Auburn, Alabama, and working in an even smaller town outside of the city, Dyesha was still getting used to their country accent. She smiled. "I'm not easily offended. My job is to get Mr. Mason out of that bed and moving again. I've created a few things that will help to speed up his recovery. Mr.

Mason, if you're willing to put forth the effort, you'll be able to get home to your wife in no time. My skin color has nothing to do with my skills that speak on my behalf."

Walt looked at Claire, then addressed Dyesha. "You've created a few things to speed up the recovery?"

"Yeah. I've created some exercises that have gotten approved, and have incorporated them into my practice. Since every patient is different, I provide therapy based upon each person's individual needs." She looked at Claire. "Mrs. Mason, I can appreciate your concern. With your husband's help, he won't need my services for long. Mr. Mason, I'll be back later to get you scheduled, if that's okay."

"Looking forward to it."

Dyesha smiled. "Great. See you later. Mrs. Mason, you have an amazing day."

As the two ladies left, Claire overheard Linda speaking, "I can't believe that racist bit..."

Walt looked at Claire and shook his head. "The lady came to help me, and you attack her?"

"I didn't mean—I mean, I thought—"

"Don't bother, Claire...Why don't you have a seat."

Claire took the chair from the wall and pulled it up to Walt's bed just as Millie, his mother, walked in carrying an apple pie in a covered container.

"Hey, hey, hey. There's my boy." She went over and kissed him on the forehead. "Look at your hair." She grabbed his chin. "And you need a shave. Don't look like they've been taking good care of you like they did at the hospital. I'll take care of that. You have to stay on 'em. You know, I worked in a nursing home for over ten years. That's how I hurt my back. Been on disability ever since." She looked at

Claire. "It's always the black ones who neglect the patients. That's all right. I know how to take care of them. I speak their language. I'm gonna sit your pie on the table. I'll be right back."

"Ma, the aid already said she's gonna clean me up tonight."

"Including a shave?"

"Including a shave."

"They better if they know what's good for 'em."

"Have a seat, Ma. Claire, grab Ma that other chair."

"I got it. I can move a chair, Walt. I ain't handicapped. It might say so on my decal, but I can do more than what I put on. Besides, Claire just got off work. No need to bother her." She put the chair on the opposite side of Walt's bed.

"Um glad you're here, Ma, 'cause what I have to say, I need you both to hear me."

"Walt, you want me to cut you a slice of pie?" Millie motioned to stand.

"Not now, Ma—not now."

Millie sat back down.

"Claire...Ma...I've changed. I've been wrong. We all have, but I reckon, y'all will have to find your own way like I did. Now, I don't know if I was dreaming, but it couldn't be a dream. Not after waking up and having the same scars and cuts I had in the dream. Only difference is my manhood's still where it's supposed to be. It was cut but only left a small scar. But the other things, same broke leg, toe got half cut off, and a bad scar on my stomach. And those marks on my back they showed me in them pictures...ain't no other way to explain them except for where I know they came from and what put 'em there. All these scars and cuts I got, I experienced them. I mean, *really* experienced them. I know they didn't come from that truck accident."

"Son, maybe—"

"Hold on, Ma, I ain't done. I got a lot more on my mind that I need to get out." Sitting up in his bed, Walt looked down at his hands. "I need a minute. I just need to figure out the best way to say it."

Claire crossed her legs.

"Son, if it's anything about what you were saying before about the pie, I asked around. That pie is an old family recipe. Comes from one of our ancestors and passed down through the generations to me, 'cause my Aunt Carol never had an interest to make it."

"Ma, did you know there used to be a pie dome for that pie plate?"

"Yeah, Ma told me it got busted. Sure wish I had that. How would you know about that? I just learned of it the other day. And what else I wanna know is how would you know about that pie? About where the recipe came from?"

"If I told you, you wouldn't believe me. I just know that the recipe didn't come from our family. It was passed down through our family, that's true, but it's not our recipe."

"If you can't tell me how you know these things, you can't expect me to believe you. That pie recipe belongs to us. Created by one of my ancestors and passed down to me. I don't know who I'm gonna pass this ancestor recipe down to since you're my one and only child and you and Claire ain't got no children. Carol, my ma's sister, never had none, and neither did their brother, Bill, who was locked up before he died. I didn't have any siblings, and I sure ain't gonna teach it to my husband's side of the family. Guess it'll die with me."

"Ma, I can have children, but I'on want that recipe."

Claire dropped her crossed legs and sat up. "What do you mean you can have children?"

"You don't want the recipe? It's a secret family recipe, boy. Passed down through the generations. Probably worth a lot of money if you were to sell it. That's it, Walt. I give it to you, and you sell it. Make us both some money."

"I ain't selling a lie, Ma."

Claire tried to get his attention. "You said you couldn't have children, Walt. How would you suddenly know that you can after coming out of a coma?"

Millie, who was always ready for a debate, tried to make sure Walt kept his eyes on her. "What do you mean it's a lie? You're calling me a liar, Walt?"

Walt turned back to Claire. "I figured it was me. Since I ain't never got a woman pregnant, I figured it was me. But I know differently now. I know I can."

Demanding his attention, Millie stood up. "Walt, you're calling your mama a lie?"

"No, Ma, I ain't saying you're lying. It ain't no lie if that's what you know to be true."

Claire stood up. "I asked you about us getting tested, but you wouldn't 'cause you said it was you, not me, who couldn't have children."

"That's what you're calling me, Walt, a liar. You're saying um lying. There ain't no other way to explain it."

"How'd you know if you can have children if you ain't never had none with another woman?" Claire wanted to know.

Walt held up his hands to the faces of each of the ladies. "Hold on. Now, just wait a minute. One thing at a time." He looked at his mother. "Now, Ma, I know you won't believe me when I tell you this...but that recipe you say come from the family, came from a slave by the name of Pearl."

"What!?" Millie's voice traveled to the hallway.

Claire took Walt's arm. "Walt, I think we need to talk about this children thing. I think it's more important than apple pie."

Millie turned her attention to Claire. "It ain't more important. Our family's recipe has been in the family for a long time. Much longer than you, Claire. And because you can't have children, it stops with me."

"It's your son who can't have children."

"My son can have children. He done told you he can. What he done did is gotten with a girl who can't produce an egg if she was a hen. You ain't had but one job as a wife, and that was to give my son children and me grandchildren so our family's recipe and Walt's name could be passed on. Our family has a rich history, and I wanted to make sure it was known. That's why I gave Walt a name from our ancestor, one that needs to be passed on. 'Cause he's with you, he can't pass on the recipe or his historial name."

"I think you meant historical. And he can't pass 'em on, 'cause he can't have no children. Don't blame me 'cause the men in your family got a low sperm count. You couldn't produce but one child and that was Walt. And all of them women he's been with, none of 'em got pregnant by your son."

"Claire, that's not called fo—"

Millie cut Walt off. "That's because they used birth control. I bet you never used it. I know about you, Claire. You were a fast gal coming up. That's probably why you can't have children. Sex with all those different boys and men done ruined you."

"You're one to talk. You ain't no saint, Millie."

"Ma."

"Don't Ma, me, Walt. You and your wife can go straight to hell." Millie walked to the table and snatched the pie dish. "Give me my pie. I ain't baking you another." She took her purse and pie and began walking out.

"Ma, sit!" He turned to Claire. "You too, Claire!"

"Um not gonna be called a liar by you, Walt. Or talked down to by your wife."

"Ma, please...have a seat."

Mumbling, Millie put the pie container and her purse back on the table and sat.

"Ma, I know this is hard to believe. It was hard for me to believe too, but I saw it. I lived it. I was there. I saw everything. You see my green eyes? I know where they come from. Your eyes ain't green. Neither is my dad's or no one else in our family. And Ma, my name. Hmp." He sighed heavily. "It came from a slave."

"From a slave? Naw...no, that's a lie! My grandma, she said where your name came from."

"I don't know what she told you, but my green eyes and my name both came from a slave named Walt. A slave who was hung for loving a White girl who loved him back."

"No, that ain't what happened. Walt blew off the head of a slave for talking back to one of my great grands."

"Walt's mother was a mixed slave who got pregnant from a slave by the name of Tondey. A very dark slave who started out like a coward but ended up a hero. When Tondey tried to tell one of your great-grands about her grandfather, who was a slave with green eyes, her mother had her husband kill 'im to bury that secret. The secret is that we are the descendants of a green-eyed slave by the name of Walt. And his father was a very dark slave named Tondey."

"You're saying I got nigger blood in my veins, is that what you're trying to tell your pearly White mama, Walt?"

"I've already told you, Ma. And that pie is the recipe of a slave by the name of Pearl. She taught one of your great-grands how to make that pie, who took the pie to be her own recipe. The same great grand who had Tondey killed. Everything you know about your heritage is a lie."

"Well, I don't believe you. I don't believe none of it. That pie recipe is my great-grand's recipe. I ain't never heard nothing 'bout some Pearl slave. Or a Tondey. What the hell kind've name is that? Where're you getting this stuff from, Walt? Who told you these lies? You dreamt it in that coma?"

Dyesha and Linda walked toward the door but stopped to listen.

"Ma, I lived it. Now, I can't explain it. At least not in no way you'll understand it, but what um saying is the truth. You raised me to hate the very thing that's keeping you alive. The blood of a Black man. That same blood is running through your veins.

"Black people ain't never did nothing to us but give us life. From Adam and Eve, they gave us life. And we hate 'em. For no-good reason, we hate 'em. We fault 'em for trying to survive the obstacles they face every day that the White man keeps putting in front of 'em. But if you knew what they've been up against, all their lives...How hard they've worked, all their lives, for free. Beaten, raped, hung, used, abused, and killed, not educated, *just* for being Black. Why, Ma? Why should I hate 'em? You taught me to hate 'em, but you never told me why I should. At least not a good reason. Tell me, why?"

"'Cause...'ca-'cause, I don't know. Just 'cause they're Black, that's why."

"That's a *no-good reason*, Ma. That's a no-good reason to hate somebody. Do you hate them, Ma? Do you have Black people?"

"Yes. 'Cause I can. 'Cause they are outgrowing us. Keep having all of them children, just like them Mexicans. They're lazy. Don't wanna work...on that welfare."

"Ma, you're on welfare."

"'Cause um disabled."

"You just said earlier, 'I ain't handicapped. It might say so on my decal, but I can do more than what I put on.' Is it all right for you to be on welfare, but no other race?"

"I won't have you fussing at me about smut Blacks, Walt."

"Smut Black, yeah, I grew up calling them the same thing because I heard you say it." He sighed heavily. "Ma, will you please leave."

With her lips balled in, Millie turned to take her pie.

"No, leave it."

"Why?"

"'Cause I'm gonna give it to the Black employees here. Let them taste it. I want 'em to taste the recipe of a slave. And who knows, maybe one of 'em is the descendant of Pearl, the slave who created the recipe."

Millie snatched up her purse and marched out of the room. Passing by Dyesha and Linda, she looked Dyesha up and down. "My son's a nigger lover. You should love him."

Claire waited for her to leave. "Walt...Um sure you had some...dreams that seemed real to you, I won't deny you that. But you're not gonna change my views about Black people."

"If that's the way you feel, then that's all that's left of us 'cause I can't be with a woman who hates people for the color of their skin.

Not when I know I have Black blood in me. That means you hate me too."

"I don't hate you, Walt."

"But you hate Black people."

"Walt, you're not Black. No matter what you've dreamed, you're not Black."

"A part of me is and um gonna get me one of those ancestor tests to prove it. Then what are you gonna do about us? Can you be with a man with Black blood in him?"

"Never."

"Well, I got news for you...you already have."

Claire took her purse and jacket from the chair and left.

Dyesha and Linda walked into the room just when Linda was getting a phone call. "I'll be right back," she said.

Dyesha went in alone and saw heaviness on Walt's face. "Mr. Mason, should I come back?"

"No, please come in. You're right on time."

Seeing his brownish hair, sand-colored face, and green eyes, she smiled. She could tell from his feet that stretched to the bed's bottom railing and from how high he sat up that he was rather tall. She stopped at the side of his bed.

"Before we start talking about physical therapy and how fast you can get me back on my feet, I have a question that will seem a little bit odd. And I know you don't know me, but I need you to trust me on this."

Dyesha immediately became curious. "Oookay."

"I don't know if you noticed how I looked at you when you came in earlier."

"I did."

"I'd like to explain why. It was because...You looked like someone I once knew...Tell me what you know about your slavery ancestors."

"Excuse me?" She crossed her arms.

"Um sorry. I know the question seems somewhat weird coming from me, but...I have some insight about a slave woman by the name of Paty, and you look remarkably like her. Almost a spitting image of her."

"Paty...that's funny."

"How so?"

"I ah...I traced my lineage *anddd* found someone in my family's bloodline by the name of Paty. I remember thinking how interesting the name was, Paty, for a slave woman. I looked up what I could learn about Paty and found that she was what we would call a Physician Assistant today. I was quite proud of that."

"You should be, but I can tell you more about Paty."

She smiled. "Really."

"Yes."

"I'd like that and would be interested in learning how you would know about her."

"Well, I'll tell you everything I know. I just don't know if you're open enough to believe what I have to tell you."

"I might surprise you."

He smiled.

Chapter 52

Later that night...

Walt couldn't sleep. He opened his eyes and hoped to see the old man in the dark corner of the room. He lifted his head and looked in that direction. "Where are you, old man?"

He hadn't seen the old man since he'd been awakened. Doubts that all he'd experienced had been a dream kept waving like a violent sea amid a raging storm. *I need confirmation.* "I need the old man to appear...to tell me it wasn't some dream." But the darkness in the room was all that accompanied him.

Walt fell asleep but woke up shortly after when something brushed against his arm. He jumped and grabbed his arm. "What?"

There was nothing in his room. He looked at his arm. The eerie feeling remained with no evidence that something other than the air in the room had awakened him. Releasing his arm, he sat up, looked around, and took in a deep breath. Leaning back, he closed his eyes and rested his mind.

Moments later, he felt another light brush against the hairs on his arm, making them stand up. His eyes swung open and landed on the old man who was only feet away from him. *You're smiling. You're actually smiling.*

Walt's cheeks raised high as he smiled. He stared until his eyes burned from the need to blink. He fought against the sensation, thinking that if he did blink—that *when* he did, "You might be gone."

He gave into the urge and blinked. When he quickly reopened his eyes, the old man's back was to him, walking away, fading into the darkness of the room until he was gone.

"That's all I needed. For you to come to me again and let me know it wasn't a dream. I guess...no, *I know* it was a lesson...a lesson that I needed to learn, to teach and to preach, and I will."

A sense of sadness pressed upon his heart. Then the loneliness lifted, leaving him with peace. Smiling again, he was happy, reborn.

A little boy took shape in his mind. One with curly hair and a bright smile. "Green eyes. Walt...I love you, son. Um gonna make you proud of me. Um gonna make up for what they did to you. What your own family did to you." He shook his head amid the tears that fell from his eyes. Um gonna make you proud, son."

Chapter 53

While on her break one day, Dyesha visited Walt's room to learn more about Paty. The two sat in the chairs in his room.

Walt couldn't help but smile when reminiscing about Paty. "She originated from France and was raised by a French doctor who may have been her father. He taught her everything he knew about medicine and taking care of sick and injured people."

"How do you know of this? Did you research it, and why? Why do research on this particular slave?"

"Research? Naw, I wouldn't even know where to begin to do research on a slave. Before this accident, I never would have wanted to. Dyesha, I was a racist. Prior to waking up from that coma, I was a proud racist. Research, no ma'am. I lived it. I was there. I was her patient."

His answer stunned her. "What do you mean, there? And that you were her patient. That was in the eighteen hundreds. During slavery."

"I know that would cause the need for an explanation. Before the coma, I tried to run over an old man. Twice. This old man, he...he did something to me. Poured some kind of smelly concoction on me.

After feeling the burn of it, the next thing I remember was waking up on a slave plantation and seeing Paty."

"And you don't think it was a dream while in a coma?"

"No. It wasn't a dream, and I have the scars to prove it." He lifted his shirt.

"Aren't those scars from the accident?"

"Some could be explained that way, but others." Still holding up his shirt, he stoodm turned his back to her, and raised his shirt up higher.

Dyesha stood to examine the scars. "Do you mind?" she asked while hovering her hand over the scars.

"Go right ahead."

Her fingers touched them reverently. "I...I recognize these kinds of scars. They're from whip lashes. And you have a lot of them, but how...Were you abused as a kid?"

"My ma only hit me once and that was a quick whack on the butt with her hand on top of my shorts. No, ma'am. I wasn't abused as a child."

"What about some sort of injury?"

"Aside from the recent car accident, never."

"But how...where did these whip lashes come from?"

He turned to face her while pulling his shirt down. "Where do you think?"

"A whip?"

"More than one whip and more than once."

"You-you want me to believe that you were beaten with a whip?"

"I know. I know it's hard to believe. After that stuff he poured on me, I woke up on a slave plantation and became Tondey, a slave. Now, I don't know how long because every time I was beaten, I passed out and ended up on another plantation, living the life of Tondey who turned out to be one of my ancestors."

"That's ah...that's an amazing story." She sat.

He sat. "I know. And I don't expect anyone to believe it. Hell, I wouldn't if I didn't have the scars to prove it. Scars that no one, not even the doctors can explain how they got there. My wife doesn't know where they came from, neither does my ma and pa. But I know. Trust me, I know. I can still almost feel every lash. I'd heard about slaves being beaten with a whip..." He shook his head, "but that pain, it's nothing you can even imagine. My mind, my body couldn't handle it."

She saw the tears well in his eyes while he spoke.

"The sound it made when the overseers pulled it back. Wanting me to hear every poop before it came across my skin, ripping it apart." He squeezed his lips as tears fell.

Tears fell from her eyes too.

He covered his mouth and sniffed. "Before this, I would have laughed to hear of this kind of abuse to a Black man." Sticking out his lips, he shook his head and broke down. "No man, no child, no woman should ever experience that kind of abuse." He cried.

She rushed to him. He allowed her to wrap her arms around his shoulders, his arms went around her hips, and he just sobbed.

"Um sorry." He took tissue from a nearby table.

She did the same before returning to her seat. "I'm so sorry you had to live through that."

"So, you believe me."

"A dream doesn't manifest itself into tangible scars. And unless you miss your calling as an actor, I don't know. I find it hard not to believe. I mean, if the scars weren't there..." She leaned forward. "Tell me more about Paty."

He smiled. "Paty. She had the most beautiful tan skin and long black straight hair that hung down her back. Her lips were full."

"That could be any Black woman."

"Yeah, but this one had a beauty mark, a mole on the side of her left nostril. I remember wondering if it was a nose piercing. And those freckles, they danced from one cheek to the other. She was so innocently beautiful. Small figure, flat breasted, medium height...beautiful, just gorgeous small feminine hands. She had fingers made for rings. She spoke proper, not like a slave, but with a slightly French accent."

"Wow, that's creepily interesting."

"I know."

Dyesha shook her head and sat up. "No, you don't understand. That description matches the old photograph I was able to find of Paty...Walt, I don't know how you could have known that unless you found the same photo. And even if you did, what's the possibility of me meeting you and you knowing about Paty? ... And you're right, I do look a lot like her." She dropped back. "I believe you. I believe your unbelievable story."

He sighed heavily. "Thank you. Sometimes I question if it was true but hearing you say you believe me, I know that it wasn't a dream. Not a dream to get to know Paty who was beautiful inside and out. She was so caring. So easy to fall in love with. And Black Bean Ray, that was her man, he truly loved her."

"Black Bean Ray. I learned that he was her husband and that they had three children. It's amazing that you know all of that. How else would you have known without research unless you were there?

I just still find it hard to believe, but I just do. I don't know why because I don't know you in that way, but I do."

Walt smiled. "Thank you. And she did marry Black Bean Ray? I'm so happy to hear that. You said they had three children?"

"Yes, three beautiful children."

"That's surprising."

"Why?"

"Because Tondey, he..." Walt explained Tondey's cowardliness to her. "But Black Bean Ray was always a forgiving man. He carried such dignity, loyalty, and respect. I aspire to be like him."

She smiled.

The next day, Dyesha walked into Walt's room, pulled something from a folder she carried and held it out to him. She paid close attention to see how he would respond.

Taking it, his mouth dropped. "Paty. This is Paty. I remember her as if it was yesterday."

Dyesha smiled. "And this one." She handed him another image.

"Wow, Black Bean Ray." Walt held the photo and stared. Flashes of their moments together colored the black and white image. "He was a good man. And this is their family."

"Yes. Paty, Black Bean Ray, and their children."

She took the images from him. "Walt, you taught me a lot about her. Let me return the favor by helping you trace your lineage. And I won't lie, I believe you, but this research may confirm all that you said you have lived. It will help me believe you unequivocally."

"Yeah, we can do that. I'd love to. I want to make sure that it wasn't a dream too. Can you start with a DNA test?"

Chapter 54

Months later...

No longer in rehab, Walt finished work, went to his room at a local hotel, and took a shower. He made sure to smell and look good before going to the small-town library where he met Dyesha. She gave him an intimate hug, and then the two smiled at each other and sat down at a table, facing her laptop.

"Guess what came in the mail today?" He handed her a large envelope.

She smiled and took it. "You didn't open it."

"No. I wanted you to open it. I was too nervous."

She pulled the letters from the envelope. "We can also see this information online, but we'll start here." She read. "Wow, look at this, you see that percentage?"

"Yeah."

"It means that you have even more African American blood in you than you thought."

After looking over the documents, she helped him understand them. "Let me show you what I found online about Tondey. I bookmarked all the pages. Look at this docket. It's the only one I could find with the name Tondey on it...Look here." She hovered the computer's cursor on a specific name. "Walt. Age ten through twelve. Mulatto. Looks like Tondey and Walt were on the same plantation."

"Which one?"

"I can't make out the name. Hold on, let me see something." She did some more digging. "Loooooks like it was the..."

"Finch Plantation."

She looked at him. "Yeah, you're right. Look, Tondey's name is here." She pointed the cursor and scrolled down. "Walt's name is there. I suppose a census was taken during the short time they were on the plantation at the same time. You're right. You two have the same name, Walt. What're the odds of that?"

"Wow. I didn't dream it. What about the Lora Dean Plantation?"

"I've been searching for that plantation all week. All I was able to find on Lora Dean's Plantation was that it was used to treat sick slaves. No names of any of the slaves and just the year Lora Dean died."

"What about a Mildred?"

"There are too many by that name...unless you have some information that's more definite, it would be impossible to find her. Who was she?"

"Walt's ma. Families were torn apart. It wasn't right." The new information was a spark that did not go out for Walt. "I have to do more."

"What can you do?"

"I wanna become an attorney."

"An attorney?" Dyesha asked.

"Yes, a civil rights attorney. But first, I have to get my high school diploma."

Chapter 55

~~ A year later... In the year 2020 ~~

The year 2020 could be said to have been the single worst year of all time. The year the COVID-19 virus came upon us. Killing and destroying the lives of people of all races, backgrounds, and ages. Many lives were ended by this pandemic that seemed to have vengeance to no end. However, for some, like Walt, January 2020 was the beginning of a happily ever after.

On New Year's, 2020, Walt sang to Dyesha as she walked down the aisle to him. He proclaimed, "I do, and I will!" to the direct and established descendant of Paty in her Pennsylvania hometown.

Prior to their nuptials, Dyesha had helped him get his GED, and when they relocated, Walt became a victim advocate while attending college majoring in law.

Dyesha immediately became pregnant following their wedding. Nine months later, she gave birth to a brown-eyed baby boy who they named Walt, Jr.

On January 9, 2021, three days after the riot at the United States Capitol, Walt watched the replay of the rioters invading the Capitol on television.

"Oh, my God." Walt snatched up the remote and froze the screen.

"What's wrong?" Dyesha was breastfeeding Walt, Jr.

"That's Roy and Claire." He sat closer to the television, unfroze and rewound it, played it forward, and froze it again. "Yep, that's them."

They listened to the news reporter. "The FBI is asking for your help. If you recognize any of these individuals who participated in the riot at the state capitol, please call the number at the bottom of the screen."

Walt grabbed his phone.

"What are you doing?"

"Calling the FBI."

Epilogue

The journey behind him was long ago. The path before him knows of no end.

Carrying a satchel on his shoulder, he wears a long black trench coat that reaches to the leather boots that shine as though they have just been glossed. With a wide brim hat that shields his eyes from the sun, he is a thin, frail old man who uses a wooden staff to support his every step.

In him wisdom constantly replenishes. Like a cup that runneth over, no spills are wasted but pour into his subjects whose destiny have been chosen to impart unforgettable lessons.

The *Life Alterer* moves on to the next subject, ready to impart an unforgettable lesson.

Share Your Thoughts

Hope you enjoyed *Life Alterer*. If so, please take a few seconds to write a positive review. Love you for it!

C. Yvette Spencer, Drama Novelist on Amazon, Facebook, Twitter, and Goodreads
C. Yvette Spencer, Drama Novelist's newsletter: c.yvettespencer@gmail.com

Scan to grab your next favorite C. Yvette Spencer's book

C. Yvette Spencer's Series
Desperate Struggles Trilogy
Book 1: "Mama Ain't Dead Yet!"
Book 2: By Any Means Necessary!
Book 3: The Struggle Just Got Real!

Khonnie & Khyle Chronicles (Coming Soon)
Book 1: Uncharted Territory
Book 2: Enjoying the Ride
Book 3: Climatic High
Book 4: From Dusk to Dawn

Twisted Lessons Collection
Be Careful What You Pray For
Confessions in the Dark
Untimely Death
Devil's Prey
Covenant Seat (Coming Soon)

African American Historical Novels
The Passer
The Story of Gloria & Sadie
Life Alterer

PENT Up Freedom Collection
Life's Reflections from a Broken Mirror (Coming Soon)

C. Yvette Spencer

Drama Novelist

www.ingramcontent.com/pod-product-compliance
Lightning Source LLC
Chambersburg PA
CBHW051542260626
47170CB00003B/1068